In The End

a novel

by Edwar

This is a work of fiction. All of the characters, organizations, events and locations portrayed in this story are either products of the author's imagination or used fictitiously.

ISBN: 1494814161

http://edwardmwolfe.com

Also by Edward M Wolfe

When Everything Changed

Devon's Last Chance

Ataraxia: Georgio Goes to Space

Fun & Games & Mass Murder

DEDICATION

Shaelee and Zachariah, thank you for putting up with a father who is always writing and never shuts up about it. I love you guys and I hope you never experience an apocalypse outside the pages of fictio

"It is forbidden to kill; therefore all murderers are punished unless they kill in large numbers and to the sound of trumpets." – *Voltaire*

Part 1

First Strike

Chapter One

"If that was World War Three, it wasn't as bad as it was cracked up to be," Jim said. Those nearest him, Josh and Hailey, said nothing.

They were on the bottom floor of a condo cabin which faced the mountain in the front and had windows on both floors facing east toward Denver in the back.

Angela, who was sitting on the other side of the room looking out through the window at a mushroom cloud on the horizon, spun her head around and said, "Are you insane?!"

Jim cocked his head and scrunched his eyebrows as he looked at her without responding.

"Millions of people are *dead*!" she shouted.

"You say that like it's a bad thing," he said, getting up from the floor and stretching his back by leaning backwards as far as he could. "I'm gonna go see if I can find a radio." He headed toward the stairs that led to the upper, street-level floor.

"You are *such* an asshole," Angela said, glaring at Jim as he walked past her.

"Because I want to find a radio? Geez, Angela. You're so hyper-critical. Calm down and think about the fact that this vacation just got extended indefinitely. How cool is that?"

"I don't believe you!" Angela turned back to the window, not wanting to see what was out there, and at the same time unable to take her eyes from it for more than a moment.

Angela had always squabbled with Jim. Any casual observer would assume that she hated him, even before the nukes struck. Jim and their friends who came to the mountain with them knew otherwise. Angela had a crush on Jim that went back to junior high. Jim always acted like he didn't notice, or if he did notice, then he didn't care.

But now, Angela didn't know what she thought of Jim. It used to be that his attitude and sick humor both infuriated her and delighted her at the same time. He was completely unpredictable, and that usually made hanging out with him fun and full of surprises. But now that disaster had struck and life as they knew it was over, she felt like he was way out of line.

She was about to yell to him as he went up the stairs to the street level part of the cabin, "Fuck off, Jim. For real this time!" But it occurred to her that maybe this was Jim's way of coping, and maybe he deserved some slack. She turned to Josh and Hailey and asked, "Can you believe him?"

Josh slowly shook his head. Hailey was leaning into Josh with her head on his chest where she had cried herself to sleep. Josh continued to gently stroke her hair and stare intently at nothing.

When Jim reached the top of the stairs, he hesitated for just a second before opening the door, thinking that he might be walking into nuclear radiation. He dismissed that thought as quickly as it came to him. The nuke was too far away to affect them here on the mountain. He was sure of it. He opened the door and sniffed the air, then smiled at his own stupidity. He wasn't going to be able to *smell* radiation.

He walked through the doorway, shutting the door behind him. He turned right, heading toward the kitchen. There were no sounds coming from the cabin, or anywhere else that he could hear. There weren't many neighbors in the area since it was adjacent to a resort that catered only to beginning skiers, but still, at any given time one might hear someone chopping firewood, or a snow-plow driving past, or cars with chains on the tires, or loud music coming from a nearby cabin.

Now, there was nothing. It sounded like it would have if Jim had woken up in the middle of the night and came into the kitchen for a snack. If he had done that, the kitchen would have been silent and mostly dark with a small amount of green light coming from the clock on the microwave. Now it was daylight. The clock on the microwave looked like nothing more than a rectangle of black glass above the control buttons. It wasn't even blinking 12:00.

He entered the kitchen and glanced around. He could have sworn he'd seen a radio somewhere in the cabin. He had. It was sitting on a dusty shelf. Now where had that shelf been?

He thought it was in the kitchen, but it wasn't. He crossed the kitchen, exited on the other side and turned into a short hall with two closed doors. One door led to a bedroom that no one was using and the other led to a laundry/utility room.

Now he remembered. The radio was sitting on a shelf above a table next to the washer and dryer. He went into the room and walked straight to the shelf. He saw that the electric cord from the radio was plugged in to an outlet. He turned the volume/power knob all the way to the right. There was no sound. He then turned the tuning knob rapidly to the right. The red tuner indicator traveled in small bursts with each flick of Jim's fingers from the 540 starting position all the way to 1600 at the other end of the spectrum and it stayed silent the whole time.

Jim wondered if the batteries were disabled while there was an AC source connected. He unplugged the radio, then turned it off and then on again. There was a small popping noise and Jim thought the radio was coming to life. But he instantly realized when he heard the second pop that the sound was coming from somewhere outside.

He turned the radio around and removed the back cover. There were batteries, but he had no way of knowing if they were good or not. Carrying the radio with him, Jim headed back to the kitchen and set the radio down on the counter next to the sink so he could search for new batteries. He heard another popping sound and this time recognized it as the sound of a small caliber pistol. *Looting, already?* Jim frowned at this thought. *No way. People can't be looting up here. Not yet, anyway.* He headed out of the kitchen, through the cabin's main room and went outside. This time he didn't think of radiation before opening the door. When he stepped outside, he sniffed the air for the scent of gunpowder.

The nearest cabin was across the road and twenty yards to his left. The air was cold and he wasn't wearing a jacket, but he didn't think of going back for one. He knew he had heard gunshots now. Three of them, and then a return to the total silence that had enveloped the mountain top.

Jim started to jog across the road to the cabin across the street. He didn't bother looking either way before crossing. It was too quiet for there to be any cars coming. There was a car in the driveway of the cabin he was approaching. Jim slowed to a walk as he reached the front door. He thought he heard something. The closer he got, the clearer the noise became. It sounded like a retarded kid moaning or whining. Jim imagined a developmentally disabled kid with a firearm. If ever there was a recipe for disaster… He mentally sang a revised version of a song by a comedienne named Julie Brown.

"Everybody run. The retard's got a gun."

He smiled, thinking this could be really fucked up and not funny at all. He hoped it was not what it sounded like.

Jim opened the storm door and started to knock on the wooden door with his knuckles. His hands were already cold and rapping on the hard wood hurt his finger bones. He grabbed the brass knocker and banged it against the metal plate a few times, then let go. The moaning/whining sound grew louder and more insistent. Jim was sure that something was seriously wrong in there. It sounded like someone might need help. He tried the doorknob. It turned in his hand. He pushed the door open and saw the source of the moaning.

There were two people inside. One was making the awful moaning noise and one was dead silent. Lying on a bearskin rug in front of the crackling, warm fireplace was a young blonde woman who Jim assumed was probably pretty hot before she took two bullets to the head.

Further from the fireplace and closer to Jim was a man lying on the ground, spinning in circles. He was bleeding from the head and looked like he was trying to walk with his right foot, while lying on his side. He would place his foot on the ground and then try to get traction. His body would spin a little on the polished wood floor and then he'd try it again. His arms lay useless on the floor. Each time he used his foot and caused his body to spin a little more counter-clockwise, he moaned, possibly in frustration, as if he was trying to do something other than spin in circles and continuously failing.

Jim said, "What the fuck are you doing?"

The man's active leg jerked as if he was startled by Jim's voice. After another partial rotation the man was able to see Jim looking down at him. He began moaning in earnest now. He looked around wildly and his eyes widened when they spotted the gun not far away from where he was, but still out of reach since he couldn't move his arms. He looked at the gun, then at Jim, and groaned two syllables. "Ooooo ee!"

He repeated this several times. Although his face was frozen in place with the left side of his mouth pulled back far enough to expose his back teeth, and the right side closed, Jim sensed the man was pleading with him. Jim saw blood dripping from the man's temple onto the floor and realized what had happened here. A failed murder-suicide.

The man on the ground spun himself until he could reach the gun with his foot, then tried to kick it toward Jim. It went in a general direction somewhat toward Jim - enough for Jim to understand what "Ooooo ee" meant. He wanted Jim to finish the job for him. "Shoot me," he was trying to plead, minus consonants.

Jim said, "Fuck you," then turned around and walked out. He was pissed off now. After what that bastard had done to the blonde woman, he didn't deserve help dying. He should suffer for killing her. He looked back over his shoulder and yelled, "Asshole."

Two

Angela was standing at the foot of the driveway, hugging herself to keep from freezing when she saw Jim emerge from the doorway. She was scared that something had happened to him and was now relieved to see that he looked unharmed. "What happened in there?"

"You don't want to know," he replied and walked past her.

"Jim! What happened?" she said, turning to follow him.

Jim stopped, turned around and said, "I told you - you don't want to know!"

"Obviously, I do want to know, Jim. That would explain why I asked you. Twice, even."

"Let's get back to the cabin. We can talk about it there. You're freezing." Jim wished he had brought a jacket, just so he could give it to her. But she was as stupid as he was for coming out in the freezing cold without one.

Jim was angry over what he had just seen, but Angela had a way of always making him feel something like compassion. Jim put his arm around Angela's waist and resumed walking back to their cabin. Angela did not resist, even though she was not happy with him.

To their mutual surprise, Angela and Jim walked into the cabin to find Josh and Hailey off of the couch and moving around, for the most part like normal people again. They were gathering their belongings and looked like they were ready to leave.

"What's going on, you guys?" Angela asked.

"We're going home," Hailey replied. "Our vacation is clearly ruined so there's no point in staying here for two weeks."

Jim looked at her and started to say something, then shook his head and headed up the stairs. "Screw it," he muttered as he went up. Angela looked at Jim and then turned back to Hailey, speechless for a moment.

"Hailey! *Everything* is ruined! That was a nuclear bomb out there. Do you hear what you're saying?"

"I understand that something terrible has happened to *Denver*. But we live in *Boise,* and we're going home. If you want to stay here and ski, that's up to you." Hailey scanned the room to see if there was anything of hers she might have missed and picked up a copy of People magazine from the end-table next to the couch. She turned to Josh and said, "I think that's everything. Are you ready?"

Josh was standing next to the front door - a center-piece between four suitcases. He nodded. His expression hadn't changed from that which he had worn on the couch as he stared at the mushroom cloud over Denver, growing, rising and expanding.

"We'll see you back in Boise, Angela." Hailey walked to the door, opened it, then turned to Josh and said, "Come on! Let's go." Josh responded like an android coming out of rest mode and picked up two of the four suitcases as Hailey opened the door. She grabbed the other two suitcases and led the way outside.

Angela followed them, saying, "You guys! Think about this! If a nuclear bomb exploded in Denver, this could be World War Three right now. It might be like this everywhere. You don't know if it's safe to go to Boise. And, my god - how are you going to get there? You're just going to drive through a radiated Denver like it's nothing? Please stop and think about what you're doing!"

Josh opened the back of his Isuzu Rodeo and hefted one suitcase in, then the other. Hailey set hers down next to Josh and he dutifully loaded those in as well. Finished with his known, immediate task, he turned and stared at Hailey as if awaiting new instructions. If Hailey said nothing, he looked as if he was prepared to stand there overnight and into the next day until commanded to do otherwise.

"Let's go!" Hailey barked. "I don't ever want to come back here." Josh robotically complied. He turned away from her and walked to the driver's side of the vehicle.

Angela thought she finally understand what was wrong with them. "Hailey!" she yelled, as the other girl opened the front passenger door. "Listen to me. You're in denial. You don't know what you're doing. And Josh is in shock. He's not thinking at all. Please come back in. At least wait until tomorrow when we might know what's going on."

Hailey slid into the passenger seat, looked at Angela and said, "Good-bye, Anj. Tell Jim I said 'thanks for ruining our vacation'," and she slammed her door shut. Angela watched as Hailey turned her head toward Josh and said something she couldn't hear. A second later the engine came to life. The small, white reverse lights came on at the back of the vehicle, and the truck backed down the drive, turning to the left when it reached the road. The brake lights flared for a second, the reverse lights went out and the truck moved forward and slowly gained speed as it headed down the mountain.

Angela stared, dumbfounded, until she could see the truck no more. "Unbelievable," she muttered to no one.

Three

Angela was still staring at the road down the hill when she heard the cabin door open. Jim came out and shut the door behind him. "Go inside. You're going to freeze." He walked past her, crossing the driveway diagonally.

"Where are you going?" she asked, realizing she would be all alone if he left.

"I'm going back for the gun."

"*What gun*!?" The fear she had just started to feel as she watched Josh and Hailey driving toward a disaster increased and her heart started beating faster. She turned around and followed him.

Jim talked as they walked. "It appears that the guy across the street flipped out when he saw the nuke and decided he and his female companion would be better off dead. So he shot and killed her and then tried to kill himself. And failed. He was alive when I left, but he may be dead now." He stopped about ten feet from the door. "Wait here. I'll just be a minute."

Angela waited. Jim was right when he had said she didn't want to know. She wished she still didn't know. And she certainly did not want to see. She wondered what the hell was wrong with people. Murder and suicide. Shock and denial. She wondered if something was wrong with her and Jim too, or were they the normal ones?

Jim pushed the front door open and immediately looked at the man who had been slowly spinning like a bug pinned to a board and saw that he had stopped moving. His eyes were open, unmoving and glassy. He had finally died from his self-inflicted gunshot wound to the head. Jim was glad. Although he hated the man for shooting his girlfriend and felt that he deserved to suffer for what he did, Jim was also slightly freaked out by the macabre scene of the man hanging on to life and trying over and over to move to the gun so he could finish the job.

Jim stepped into the room and pulled the door shut behind him in case Angela's curiosity won out over her fear and caused her to peek inside. He walked across the hardwood floor, making a wide berth to the left of the dead man. He picked up the small, silver gun. It was heavier than he thought it would be. He examined the left side and saw a small tab above a red dot and he pushed the tab downward, concealing the dot. The gun's safety was now engaged. He reached behind himself and slipped the gun into the back pocket of his Levi's.

He had only come for the gun, but now that he was here, in an "empty" house, he felt that he should check if there might be other useful items he should take as well. He walked into the adjoining kitchen/dining room area and glanced around. There was an open laptop running on the table against the wall. He stepped closer and looked at the screen. The only program running was a web browser which was at a do-it-yourself stock trading website. Jim shutdown the laptop, closed the lid and put it into the empty carrying bag that was on the floor beneath the table. He didn't know if he'd ever need it or not, but it was an expensive laptop without an owner and it didn't make sense to leave it behind. He zipped the case shut and set it down on top of the table to grab on his way out.

Jim stood still in the silent cabin and tried to think of what else he should even look for. He thought of the circumstances he was facing. A nuclear weapon had exploded in Denver. There was no power. He and Angela were stranded on top of a mountain for an indefinite period of time. Josh and Hailey had driven away in the SUV. They had a week's worth of food, but even less if you discounted anything that needed to be cooked - especially in the microwave or electric oven. That gave him an idea. He started looking in cabinets near the stove hoping to find some Sterno, but there was nothing but cookware and a few seasonings.

Jim decided this was a task better suited for two people. He left the kitchen, crossed the living room, and again steered wide around the dead yuppie and went to the other side of the cabin where there was a small hallway with one door on each side. He picked the room on the left for no reason and pulled the comforter off the bed. The pillows came with it and fell to the floor as he bundled the comforter up against his chest. He walked to the main room and covered the body of the young woman. He went to the other room, found it also had a bed and took that bed's comforter and used it to cover the man.

He walked the few steps over to the front door and opened it. Angela was standing there with her back to the door lifting one foot and then the other, walking in place to try to generate some warmth. Even with Jim's jacket on, she was cold and every breath she took was visible in the frigid air. "I need some help in here," he said to her back.

"Jim, I don't know if I can - "

He cut her off. "I took care of that. Come on." He reached for her shoulder and gently pulled her toward him. She came in slowly, taking small steps through the doorway, afraid of what she might see. She looked at the floor, first at one blanket with a body shape beneath it, then the other.

"Is that - are those...?

Jim's hand was still on her shoulder and he used it to turn her toward the hallway with the two bedrooms. The man's body was now behind her but the woman's was still to her left, easily visible in her peripheral vision. He pulled her toward the hall and this time she didn't hesitate to start walking. "I want you to look through their suitcases, or backpacks - whatever they have - for anything you think might be useful. Also check the bathroom in the master bedroom on the left. Shampoo, razors, toothpaste - anything like that.

"We're robbing them?" she asked, sounding alarmed and opposed to the idea.

"We are *not* robbing them. They're dead. They don't own anything. We're gathering -"

"Okay, so we're looting. Whatever you call it, it's still wrong."

Jim took a deep breath and told himself to be patient and keep his voice level. "Listen to me, Angela. I'm trying to think ahead here. We don't know how long we're going to be without power or any kind of services. We have no vehicle to go to the market for food or supplies. We sure as hell can't risk hiking or hitching a ride into Denver after what just happened. We have no cell signal. We're kinda stranded with a limited amount of food, and this cabin, at least, has supplies that the former occupants won't be needing.

We have to survive, and we don't know for how long. If we don't take what's available here, someone else will. Sooner or later, it's bound to happen. So let's think about ourselves and our immediate survival for now and we can map out a revised moral code later. Will you help me?"

"I'm sorry. You're right. I just didn't think about... I haven't really..."

"It's okay. Just see what you can find. Anything that you would want to buy if it was sitting on a store shelf - put it in a bag or suitcase. I'm gonna see what they have for food. Okay?"

Angela looked around the hallway and into the master bedroom then back at Jim. She said, "Okay." Jim pulled her close to him and put his arms around her. She hugged him tight and whispered, "Jim, I'm so scared. I don't know what I would do right now if you weren't here."

"It's okay," he said softly with his mouth beside her ear. "I'm here."

Four

It took them two trips to carry back the things they had gathered. They both went back once more to make sure there was nothing else. They stepped out of the cabin empty-handed, satisfied that they had gotten everything that might be useful. Jim turned around to lock the door with the keys he had taken from the male corpse. Angela was looking across the road and through the trees.

"Jim, what's that? Oh my god!"

Jim immediately thought another nuke had hit and quickly turned around. "What? Where, Angela? I don't see anything."

"Right there," she said, pointing at nothing but trees as far as Jim could tell. "Look at the roof of our cabin, then look to the left through the gap between the branches."

"Oh shit." Jim saw what she was looking at. There was a small figure dangling against the backdrop of the winter sky, swinging his legs back and forth. "God dammit!"

"What's wrong?" Angela asked.

"There's a guy stuck on a ski lift!"

"I know. But why did you curse?"

"Because now we have to go rescue the poor bastard."

"Is he a skier?"

"Can't be. The resort isn't open for a few more days, but it's definitely someone on a ski lift. Must've got stranded when the power went out."

"Jim, we've got to help him!"

Jim handed Angela the keys he was holding and said, "Start this car and turn on the heater. I'm gonna go lock our cabin and be right back." Angela took the keys and hesitated. She knew there was no reason not to use a car that no longer belonged to anyone, but she still had a feeling that it wasn't right.

Jim ran across the street and Angela looked at the keys in her hand, easily identifying the button that unlocked the BMW in the driveway. She unlocked the door and got in the driver's seat. She looked for an ignition to the right of the steering wheel and found a button where she expected to put the key. The button had the words "START" and "STOP" written on it. Not sure if it would work or not, she pushed the button and was a little startled when the engine came to life.

She looked at the keys in her hand, then out the window toward her cabin and saw Jim coming back, heading toward the driver's side of the car. She pulled her legs up and moved over to the passenger seat. Jim got in and asked, "Did you turn on the heater?"

Angela looked at the dash console and said, "No, but I think it's already on. All I did was push that button and the car started right up. What's to keep people from stealing expensive cars like this?"

"What do you mean? Any car can be stolen." He put on his seatbelt and backed out of the driveway.

"Well, it seems like if you can get in this car whether the doors were unlocked or you just broke a window, you don't even have to hot-wire it; you just push a button and it starts."

"Oh, that." He shifted to Drive and headed down the hill. "If you didn't have the fob, the button wouldn't do anything. There's a microchip in the fob that the car's sensors read, which then unlocks everything like turning a key to the On position."

"That's really cool. You probably think it's dumb, but I'm always amazed by modern technology. We really do live in the space age, ya know?"

"Yeah. Technologically, we're advanced beyond anything we should be allowed to possess."

Angela was about to ask Jim what he meant by that, but then she thought of nuclear weapons and assumed that's what Jim was referring to. Jim turned the car at a corner where a sign directed drivers to the Ice Bunny Ski Lodge.

"We're like monkeys on crack, with laser guns," Jim said as he shifted the car into Low for the steep incline up to the lodge.

Five

They parked next to a maroon Chevy pickup that was the only other vehicle in the lot. There was a row of ten cabins in front of them and a large main lodge building behind them. Jim said, "Stay here and keep warm."

"I'm going with you," Angela responded.

"No, you're not, Angie. You'll freeze your feet off. Have you ever walked up a ski slope? There's no reason for both of us to suffer. If you want to do something, see if you can get inside the lodge and find some food and start a fire. If I can actually get this guy down, he's gonna be frozen. And depending on how long he's been up there, he might be starving too."

As usual, she couldn't argue with Jim's logic. She wasn't happy about being left alone, but she understood that she'd be far more useful staying behind. Jim removed the skis from the rack on the BMW while Angela stood watching. She didn't know why, but watching him leave made her feel sad and she fought the urge to cry.

Jim turned around, looked at her face and asked, "What's wrong?"

"I don't know," she answered. "Just… be careful and hurry back, okay?"

"Sure," he said, wondering what was up with her. "Wait!" he said. "I need your help with something. Come here for a sec."

Jim removed his arms from his jacket and explained to Angela how he wanted her to tie his sleeves together just below the ski bindings as he held them against his back. She tied the sleeves in a knot then he asked her to zip up the front of his jacket, which she did.

"Thanks. Now I can use two poles to help me get up the slope instead of one."

Angela was still standing close to him after zipping up his jacket. She leaned forward and kissed Jim on his lips. Then she quickly turned and headed toward the lodge without saying anything.

"Huh," Jim said as he watched her walk away. He turned around and began walking across the parking lot toward the base of the run. When he reached it, he looked up and was glad to see that the guy had gotten stuck above one of the easiest of the beginner runs. It wasn't going to be hard at all to reach him on foot.

Jim never said anything on his way up the slope; not even when he was sure he could be heard. He waited until he was almost directly beneath the man before he yelled up to him. "Need some help!?"

The man was startled out of his daze and looked down at Jim who was walking to a point in front of him now. "If you're not too busy, sure. I could use a hand," he replied.

Jim liked him immediately. "You probably have a better idea than I do about how to get you down. What would you like me to do?"

The man said, "If you could walk the rest of the way up to the terminal, there's a diesel engine that'll get this thing moving again since the power's out."

"Got it!" Jim said and resumed his uphill journey. A short while later, Jim watched the man slowly moving up the slope as the smell of burning diesel spread out around him. The man hopped off the chair with a smile, stuck out his hand and said, "I'm Terry. I owe you one for saving my ass." Jim shook his hand and told Terry he didn't owe him anything. Anyone would have done it.

"Maybe you're right, but the way I see it, the resort doesn't even open for another few days, so I'm damned lucky you happened to be here. What brought you over, anyway?"

"You did. A friend of mine spotted you dangling on the line and pointed you out to me. So I guess you are kinda lucky, but if you want to thank someone, that would be Angela. Should we take the lift back down, or do you want to ski down?"

Terry said it would be best to shut off the lift and ski down, so they did. When they stepped through the front door to the lodge, they could smell an unusual combination of hot dogs and coffee. "I guess you're not as lucky as we thought," Jim said.

Angela stepped out of the kitchen and into the main room. "You made it! You must be hungry and freezing. I've got some hot coffee ready for you."

"And hot dogs?" Jim asked, sniffing the air.

"Everything's frozen. I didn't know how much time I'd have to thaw anything out, so I made hot dogs. I guess I could've made soup instead. Sorry."

"I skipped breakfast this morning and spent the entire day hanging in the breeze, so right about now, hot dogs sound great. Coffee too. Thank you!"

The three of them sat in the dining area at a table big enough for eight. Angela had started a fire in the huge fireplace and the only sounds for a few moments were of wood crackling and the slurping sound one makes when trying to drink off the top of a cup of coffee that is too hot to sip quietly.

"So," Jim finally said. "Did you see a big flash this morning?"

"I figured that must've been a transformer blowing, which stranded me."

"One or more transformers may have blown, but I have much worse news for you. We got nuked."

Terry choked on the food he was swallowing and his face started to turn red. Jim jumped up and ran to him. He pulled Terry's chair out, put his arms around the man and did the closest he could come to a Heimlich maneuver. Terry expelled the food that was caught in his throat and looked briefly at Angela and then away. Still coughing and trying to regain his composure, he covered the food he spat out with a paper towel. "Sorry," he said between coughs.

When he stopped coughing, he wiped his watering eyes and looked at Jim. "That makes twice now." Jim walked back to his seat and resumed eating, waving off Terry's gratitude.

"Did you say we were nuked? That would explain why the flash seemed to come from every direction at once. I thought it was just snow-flash. Or maybe I just wanted to find an ordinary explanation for something that didn't have one."

"Yeah, we were nuked. And that's all we know. It could have just been Denver, but it could be everywhere. Our radio wouldn't work after we saw the flash, so we don't have any news. Have you got one here we can try - if they're not all dead from EMP."

"The one I was listening to this morning in the walk-in cooler might still work. But isn't that your BMW parked next to my truck?"

"Sorta," Jim replied.

Terry looked at Jim and raised his eyebrows as if asking how the car was "sorta" his.

"It's a loaner. Long term."

Terry decided the details of the car's ownership didn't matter. "If you were able to drive it, we either didn't have an EMP blast, or it's shielded, which would be really unusual for the average car. Did you happen to borrow it from someone who works at NORAD?"

"I borrowed it from a dead neighbor."

"Oh," replied Terry. "Then it might just be that the power station in Denver was knocked out. I'll go grab my radio. Be right back."

Terry got up and went off in a hurry toward the kitchen.

Jim ate the last of his hotdog and started looking around the room. "Did you notice if they have any cigarettes here?" he asked Angela.

"Why? You don't smoke."

"I do now."

"Why, Jim? You haven't smoked since high school."

"I don't know, Angela. Maybe because I'm not so concerned about my health since a nuclear bomb just went off downtown. Jesus. Don't hassle me, just answer the question."

"There's a vending machine by the restrooms."

"Thank you. Where are the fucking restrooms?"

Angela frowned and pointed back over her shoulder with a thumb. Jim got up and walked in the opposite direction of where she had indicated. "Where are you going? I thought you wanted cigarettes."

"I do. But I don't have any coins." He walked over to the cashier's counter and began pushing buttons on the cash register. He started hitting the buttons harder, then he kicked the counter.

"Is it on?" Angela asked. "There should be a key."

Jim looked more closely at the cash register, saw the key and noted that it was in the OFF position. He turned it to the setting that said SALES then started hitting buttons again with no better results.

Angela sighed, got up and walked over to him. She pressed a button and the drawer popped open as the cash register dinged. Jim grabbed a roll of quarters from the far left compartment of the coin drawer and headed toward the restrooms. "Thanks, shweetheart," he said in something like a Humphrey Bogart voice.

"Hey!" she called out. He looked back at her with his eyebrows raised. She said, "Get me some too." Jim made a sound like a small amount of air being released from a tire stem.

"Oh, it's okay for you to smoke, but not for me?"

Jim didn't answer. He disappeared into the dark corridor where the restrooms and vending machine were. He came back a few minutes later and tossed a pack at Angela who was still sitting at the table.

"What are these?" She said, looking at the unfamiliar cigarette pack in an off-silver package.

"Cigarettes, dumb-ass. What you asked for."

"I *know* they're cigarettes, Jim. I meant, what brand. I've never seen these before." She took a deep breath and silently encouraged herself to ignore Jim's attitude. He *really* wasn't a jerk, she told herself. He just acted like one - perfectly.

Jim and Angela opened their cigarette packs; neither of them thinking about the fact that being non-smokers, they did not have lighters or matches. Jim realized first and got up from the table. As he started walking toward the kitchen, he almost ran into Terry coming out.

"Have you got a light?

"No, but there are long stick matches by the grills."

"Thanks." Jim walked past him and into the kitchen. Terry went back to the main room carrying his radio and smiling. Angela saw the radio and Terry's smile and she smiled in return.

"It works?"

"I think it will. I think the cooler shielded it - if there was an EMP."

"Great! So the batteries are still good."

"Actually, no. I didn't have any batteries. I was using A/C this morning."

"Oh." Angela's smile dropped away. With no power and no batteries, the excitement of the radio was now lost. "Maybe we can find some batteries," she said, afraid to hope.

"No need. Watch this."

Terry and Angela heard Jim coughing and turned to look toward the kitchen. Jim came walking toward them, coughing and smiling, enjoying his smoke despite the trouble he was having getting used to it again.

Terry turned a knob on the bottom right side of the radio and a green LCD panel lit up. Angela's eyes lit up also. "You *do* have batteries!"

"Nope."

"Oh, come on. You have to. The radio is on."

"Nope. No batteries. You see that mirror over there?" Terry pointed to his left at a mirror on a wall.

Angela squinted her eyes and frowned, wondering what the mirror had to do with anything. "Yes," she said.

Jim sat down next to her, took a cigarette from her pack and lit it with the end of his own, then handed it to her. She took it, but just held it, still looking at Terry.

"And you see that one over there?" Terry pointed to another, larger mirror on his right.

"Yeah?"

"And you know what happens when you look at the reflection of one mirror in another mirror, right?"

"Well, yeah. They keep reflecting each other for as far as you can see."

"Exactly. It's called the Infinity Effect. Wherever you have an Infinity Effect, you have a particle wave, which carries energy. With this radio between the two mirrors, there's enough energy generated by the Infinity Effect to power the transistors."

Angela looked from one mirror to the other, then to the radio and back to Terry. "That's amazing! I never heard of that."

Jim couldn't hold it any longer and burst out laughing. Angela looked at him, wondering what was so funny.

"What?" she said.

Jim took a drag from his cigarette and started coughing again. Between coughs, he was still laughing.

Terry smiled and said, "I'm just kidding with you. The battery is charged by a hand-crank. I charged it before I brought it out here. That's what took me so long."

Despite the disaster of that day, and the possibly bleak future they all faced, the three of them laughed briefly for the first time in a while.

The men laughed a little louder, and a little longer.

Six

After several minutes of tuning through nothing but static, Terry finally gave it a rest. "Well, we still don't know anything."

"But if there are no radio stations broadcasting, doesn't that mean there had to be an EMP?" Angela asked Terry.

"Not necessarily. The stations probably don't have any electricity either. There could be too much electro-magnetic interference in the air for the signals to get through. Or an EMP may have hit Denver and the surrounding areas but not made it up this high."

Jim lit another cigarette. "I thought nukes had to be detonated high in the atmosphere to create an EMP."

"They can be, for greater effect, but they don't have to be. Depends on how smart the attackers were and what their intentions were. We have no idea who even hit us or why."

"I just thought of something!" Angela and Terry both turned toward Jim. "We came up here with some friends who left after the nuke went off. They were driving their SUV which couldn't have been shielded. At least I don't think it was - they bought it new from a dealer in Nampa."

"You're probably right," Terry said.

"Either way, we have no power, so I don't see what difference it makes," Angela replied.

She got up and started gathering the plates. Terry scooted his chair back, making more room for Angela. He looked at her and said, "It actually makes a huge difference. If the power station is just knocked out, then it can presumably be brought back online fairly soon, depending on how bad the damage is. But if it was an EMP, it could be years before we see electricity again - especially if this is happening all over the country.

"And if most of the population is dead, we're gonna be running low on electrical engineers who can get the power back on."

Angela froze, looking at Jim. "Do you think…?"

Terry reached over to Angela, putting a hand on her arm. "Hey, don't worry. We have no idea what's happened yet. Jim's just considering a worst-case scenario."

"We could be the last people alive, for all we know." Jim took a long drag from his cigarette and attempted to blow smoke-rings into the light hanging over the table.

Terry looked at him and shook his head. Angela set the stack of three plates down on the table and sat down, looking at the two men and fearing that what Jim said could be true but waiting to see what Terry would say.

"That's highly unlikely. In fact, I'd be willing to bet it's impossible. *We're* alive. And I was outside on a ski-lift when the nuke hit, so I'm sure there are plenty of people alive." Angela felt relief at hearing Terry's viewpoint and she looked at him, waiting for more reassurance.

Terry saw her need and continued. "Let's look at what we *do* know. Five of us up here are just fine. Denver is probably toast, as well as NORAD and Peterson, if it wasn't just stupid terrorists. It's possible that NORAD was the actual target so they could knock out our air defenses in preparation for a longer and larger conventional attack still to come. The rest of the entire country might be just fine."

"Except for possibly being under a conventional attack, of course."

Terry looked at Jim and began to re-assess his opinion of him. He seemed like a smart and likeable guy, but now Terry was thinking he could be difficult to be around for extended periods of time. He certainly wasn't one for keeping morale up in a crisis.

"Again, we don't know the status of the rest of the country, so there's not much use in speculating. For now, we should consider some basic possibilities and then make some plans on how we can deal with the most likely scenarios."

"What do you mean?" asked Angela.

"Well, take the power for instance. If we're going to be without power for a few months, we need to think about preserving the food we have here, and being able to stay warm through the winter while we wait for the power to come back on."

"And if the power isn't coming back on for years?" Jim asked, always the optimist.

"Then we need to plan on moving somewhere. We have plenty of food to get us through this winter, but when that runs out, we're going to need to be able to grow our own. And this ain't the place to do it."

"Oh, god," Angela said and buried her face in her palms, suddenly overwhelmed with the realization that life as she knew it might be forever lost. She had no idea how to grow food or where a good place to do it would be. She conjured up an image of a farm in her mind, and then an old, foot-powered sewing machine, and then visualized herself wearing a homemade *Little House on the Prairie* dress.

Terry patted her arm and said, "Remember, we don't know anything yet. It might not be that bad at all. Don't go thinking the worst just yet. For all we know, the power could be back on in a week and things could be back to normal in no time. It's possible that this was just a lone jihadist who hit nothing but Denver. In that case, Denver would be evacuated, but life would still be totally the same for you in Nampa."

"Boise," Angela said, suspended now between fear of the worst and hope for the best.

"Okay, Boise," said Terry.

"Same thing," Jim replied.

"The people in Boise may not even know that anything has happened here. They could end up watching the news tonight and hear that disaster struck in Colorado."

"Okay, so we don't know anything except that we don't have power, our cars work, and we've got plenty of frozen food that is thawing right now."

"Right," Terry agreed. "That's what we need to focus on right now." Angela lifted her face from her hands and carefully wiped tears from her eyes. "The first thing we need to do, no matter what the extent of the situation may be, is to secure the food."

"Snow," Jim said.

"What?" Angela asked him.

Terry replied, "It's freezing outside. We need to move the food outside to keep it cold."

Jim and Terry discussed the best way to store the food that would keep it frozen but safe from animals and still be readily accessible. As they were discussing this, they heard the sound of a car pulling into the parking lot, and then the sound of the engine died.

They had visitors.

Seven

Terry and Jim ran to the windows facing the parking lot. Looking through the blinds, Jim said, "It's Josh and Hailey."

"Your friends?"

"Yeah. They said they were going home to Boise."

"Really? Denver got nuked and they decided to drive through the blast-zone?"

"We tried telling them they were crazy, but crazy people never listen. What the fuck are they doing just sitting there?"

"Maybe it's not them."

"It is. You see that Obama bumper-sticker? If you look close, you can see where I drew a Hitler mustache on it. They never noticed." Jim started to laugh, thinking about what he'd done and then stopped when the passenger side door opened. "They're getting out."

Angela joined the men at the window. "The snow doesn't look right."

"That isn't snow. It's ash," Terry replied.

"You mean fall-out?" Jim asked.

The driver-side door opened. Both front doors of the vehicle were now open, but no one emerged from either side.

"What the fuck are they doing?"

The three of them stood there staring, waiting and wondering. Finally Hailey stepped out of the vehicle and fell to the ground.

"Something's wrong. I've got to go help her," Angela said as she started toward the door. Terry grabbed her and held her back.

"You can't go out there!"

"I have to! They're my friends."

"That ash that's falling like snow is poison. It could kill you. It looks like your friends are already suffering from severe exposure. They either got out of their SUV somewhere, or it got in through the windows or vents.

Outside, Josh slowly got out of the vehicle and held onto the ski rack with his left hand, trying to steady himself. Both of them were slowly getting coated with falling ash.

"They're getting more on them. I have to get them out of it." Angela tried to pull away from Terry who was still holding on to her.

"Angela, you can't go out there. You'll get sick and probably die. I'm sorry, honey. There's nothing you can do. It's too late for them. Their only hope would be if they took off their clothes and were completely rinsed off before they came in, and that's not even remotely possible. I think it's far too late anyway. They still wouldn't stand a chance."

"How do you know? You're not a doctor! Let me go!" Angela struggled but Terry held her firmly and looked to Jim for help. Jim came over and put his arms around Angela. Terry let go.

"Angie. He's right. They're so far gone, there's nothing we can do."

Angela wrapped her arms around Jim, buried her head in his chest and cried. She knew he was right. She just couldn't stand the thought of seeing her friends outside dying right in front of her eyes and not doing anything to help them. Terry walked over to the door and turned the handle of the dead-bolt, locking Josh out, in case he made it that far.

Josh slowly made his way to the end of the car and continued walking toward the cabin door, stopping once to vomit. As he staggered slowly toward the door, Jim saw dark liquid running out of the bottom of Josh's pants and onto his white shoes.

Josh eventually made it to the door and collapsed onto the welcome mat.

"Help!" he cried out. "We need help."

"Oh, god! I can't stand this," Angela said. Jim moved away from the window and led her to the kitchen.

"Help! Please!" They could still hear Josh calling out from the other side of the door until they entered the kitchen and Jim shut the door behind them. Terry stayed where he was, thinking that Josh might try to break a window to get in, but then considered that to be unlikely as he heard Josh go into a coughing fit, followed by terrible vomiting. Then he was silent.

Terry looked over at the ash-covered heap lying next to the SUV. Hailey hadn't moved once since falling out of the vehicle. He was pretty sure that she was dead. Just then it appeared that she started to cough and then she stopped as her throat and mouth filled with vomit. Her body spasmed briefly, causing ash to tremble and fall away from her clothing and hair, and then she was still again.

"Now she's dead," Terry said.

"L'Enfer, c'est les autres." - Jean-Paul Sartre
"Hell is other people."

Part 2

Hell on Ice

Chapter One

It rained the night that Josh and Hailey died and it continued raining almost non-stop for the next three days. Terry said it was exactly what they needed to wash away the radioactive ash that coated everything outside. They did not have a Geiger counter to see if it was safe to go out, but they assumed and hoped that it was because they needed to do something with Josh's and Hailey's bodies.

When the rain stopped falling and a light snowfall began, Terry drove his truck over to the maintenance building and came back with shovels, tarps, plywood, hammers and nails. Jim went out to help him, saw the cargo and asked, "Are we seriously going to make coffins?"

"We've got two immediate concerns: Dead bodies and food preservation. So…"

"So we're gonna eat them," Jim deadpanned.

At first Terry didn't get what Jim was saying. Then he got it and laughed, despite how macabre it was and the grim task they had ahead of them.

"No, we're not gonna eat them! Jeez. We're gonna bury them. But we also need to make an outdoor freezer for the stuff that's thawing out. At first I was thinking, "use it or lose it" but then I figured we're talking about a lot of food here, and we'd be fools to just lose it."

"So we're making a freezer out of wood?"

"Well, yes. Sort of. First, we build a box. Then we pack snow around the box, and that oughta work to keep the food cold during the day. And it'll protect it from predators. I just wish I had some hinges. It'd make it easier to get in and out of."

Jim glanced around and said, "We have plenty of hinges."

"Where?"

"On all of the doors in all of the motel rooms."

"They don't call 'em motel rooms, but yeah, you're right. We can take some from a bathroom door. Why didn't I think of that?"

"Cuz you're old and feeble, and occasionally get stuck on ski lifts."

"Okay, youngster, I'll hold the boards and you can do the nailing. Being that I'm old and feeble, I'm liable to miss the nail and smash your fingers."

The men laughed and continued to tease each other as they constructed their refrigerator box behind the lodge kitchen. By the time they had finished, there was still a light snow falling, but not enough accumulation near the lodge to pack around the box they had built. That also meant the ground was not too frozen to dig two graves.

After building the refrigerator box, they didn't have enough wood to make coffins, but they had plenty of tarps and duct tape they could use. They agreed to not tell Angela how the bodies were buried - unless she specifically asked.

It was dark before they finished digging the graves so Terry retrieved a lantern he had brought from the supply garage. Once they had light again, they finished the second grave, then the men gently lowered the bodies into the separate graves.

"Do you wanna say something?" Terry asked Jim, not knowing that Josh and Hailey were more Angela's friends than his. Being that Josh and Hailey were Jewish, the only thing that came to Jim's mind was, "L'chaim" but he decided to keep his warped humor in check out of respect for Angela.

"We'll save it for the service," he replied instead.

Surprised at himself for not even thinking of what would have ordinarily been obvious, Terry said, "Oh, right. Good idea."

Two

They held a funeral service the next day, then moved their refrigerator box behind the kitchen and packed as much fresh snow around it as they could. Then they transferred the food from freezer and the walk-in cooler. That evening they went on what Angela called "raids," but what Jim insisted were "supply runs" in the cabins near theirs.

Terry made a long list that included items Jim hadn't thought of when he and Angela had scavenged the cabin across the street from theirs. Jim and Angela thought some of the items were strange, but they didn't ask questions.

He advised them that the list was not exhaustive or exclusive. They should grab anything else they thought might be useful, but he wanted them to specifically get those items. Angela thought they should go in separate vehicles so they could cover twice as many houses in the same amount of time, but Terry insisted it was not safe for them to be separated. He didn't say why he thought it was unsafe; he just insisted that they both go in his truck. Angela felt that the biggest threat they faced was boredom, but she didn't argue.

Terry didn't say what he would be doing while they were away, but they couldn't miss seeing his handiwork upon their return six hours later. Terry had sawn multiple bathroom doors into pieces that fit over all of the lodge windows. When Jim saw what Terry had done, he just nodded. Made sense. Angela hated it.

"Now it looks condemned!" she said.

"But it's more secure," Jim replied.

Angela continued to complain as they went inside and got Terry to help them bring in their haul of supplies. "What are we secured *from* – the sun?"

"I'll explain after we unload the truck," Terry said.

A half hour later they were standing inside the lodge looking at the big pile of items they had brought in. Now they had the task of separating and storing. Terry and Jim began making separate piles of stuff while Angela cooked. A short time later, she came out with a large serving plate loaded with hamburgers, toppings and a bag of potato chips. They all sat down at the large dining table to rest, eat and talk.

"I know I haven't explained what I'm thinking or why I'm doing what I'm doing, but to be perfectly honest, I'm not entirely sure myself. I'm just wingin' it."

Angela said, "I understand the supplies. Jim had us do the same thing - right after the bomb. It was good thinking. I know I wouldn't have thought of it. But I don't understand the windows being boarded up."

The amount of light coming in through the two skylights was fading. Dusk outside meant dark inside. "If one of you will start a fire, I'll tell you where my head is at – as soon as I grab some coffee."

Jim got up and worked on starting a fire, and then he and Angela sat on the floor near the fireplace and waited for Terry to come back. After Terry boiled water for instant coffee, he returned dragging a chair behind him. He put it where the others were sitting and sat down.

"You may have noticed, I've been checking the radio for any kind of signal at least once a day. So far, I ain't got nothin'. That's a bad sign. Really bad." He looked at Jim who looked back at him, waiting for him to go on. He looked at Angela and she had a question, as he suspected.

"Why? We know the power is out, so it makes sense that no one is broadcasting."

"How much do you know about short-wave radio?"

"Um... nothing."

"Here's the thing - it ain't just local. It's national, and when the conditions are good, which is most of the time, it's international."

"Oh. That's bad. Nothing from anyone, anywhere?"

"Now you see where I'm comin' from. We should be hearing something. But we're not, and I'm no expert, but I can only think of two reasons why. First, and I don't think this is likely, but it could mean that things are bad all over the world. Second, and this is what I'm hoping - the signal just ain't getting through to us because of electro-magnetic interference, either here or somewhere else. If that's the case, it should clear soon and we'll hear from somebody. Maybe even find out what's going on."

"Does this have anything to do with the boards on the windows?" Angela asked, hoping it wasn't a stupid question.

"It does."

Jim struck a stick match on the hearth and lit a cigarette. Terry thought of saying something about the wastefulness of using an irreplaceable match while sitting next to a fire but decided to wait until after he'd addressed the subject of their resources.

"We don't know what's happened with the rest of the country, or the world for that matter, but we do know what happened in Denver. A lot of people were killed when the bomb went off. And even more will have died from radiation since then."

"Like Josh and Hailey," Angela said, quietly.

"Yes. Like them, and worse; slower, with more suffering along the way. But what we need to be concerned with is the survivors. Most folks don't have but a few days to a week's worth of food in their homes at any given time. When they run out, they'll have to forage. Only the fools will forage in town. The smart ones will look on the outskirts. Someone really smart is gonna think of this resort which was fully stocked for the season that would have begun the weekend right after the explosion."

"So the boarded windows are to keep people out?" Angela wasn't sure she understood.

"Well, first I'm hoping that if people see the place boarded up, they'll think the resort wasn't going to open for the season and therefore doesn't have any supplies. I know that's a long-shot - more likely to fool people not from around here, but the second purpose is to help keep people out who are intent on getting in no matter what."

"If someone was lucky enough to survive in the first place, why wouldn't we just welcome them in? I understand why we have to raid, but I'm not going to be a hoarder and a shut-in too."

"Survival, Anj," Jim said and flicked his cigarette into the fire. "We can't take in anyone and everyone who comes along. The more people we have, the quicker we run out of food."

"But we have more than enough to get us through the winter. That means we have plenty to share too."

"We're looking at more than just the winter, sweetheart. Once that food's gone, there's a chance that there won't be any more." Terry looked at them for a few seconds, hesitant to bring up his next topic. "We haven't talked about this yet, and I wouldn't be surprised if you two haven't even thought about it, but if we decide to stay together come spring, we'll need to find a place to grow food. And we'll need something to eat between planting and harvesting seasons. I don't think we have near enough food to take us that far - if we decide to stick together."

Angela looked at Jim. "If we have to be all survivalist and live like this all the time, we'd all do it together, right? It doesn't make sense for us to split up."

"Sure. I hate people in general, but you guys are cool with me."

Angela shook her head in mild dismay at Jim's standard line about not liking people. He had always talked as if people were a blight on the planet and she never did understand what his issue was with people. She knew he'd had a rough childhood, but she didn't think the whole world should be indicted because of a few bad people in his youth.

"I think we definitely stand a better chance of surviving well as a group than we do as individuals, and I'd be honored to be part of a continued group with you youngsters."

"Good," Angela said. "Then that's settled. We'll stick together until *surviving* isn't an issue."

"And that brings us back to the topic of other survivors who might not be as civilized as our small group is," Terry said, bringing them back to the unsettled issue of defense. "You guys brought back plenty of guns and ammo from the houses that you searched for supplies. Do you have any experience with guns?"

Jim lowered his eyelids and said in a baritone voice, "I shot a man in Reno."

Terry asked, "Just to watch him die?"

"Yep," Jim replied, hooking his thumbs into his belt loops.

"This isn't funny, you guys.

"You're right, Angela. This is a dead-serious topic. I'm sorry," Terry said.

"And no, I've never shot a gun, and I don't want to. You guys can be the sheriffs and I'll be the dispatcher. I'm *not* learning to shoot."

"I'll teach her," Jim said.

Angela responded non-verbally, pursing her lips and shaking her head defiantly.

Three

Three days earlier

Tori and her three year old daughter Elizabeth were heading back to Denver after visiting Tori's sister, Kelly in Salinas, Kansas. Just before reaching the northward curve of I-70, Tori saw a mushroom cloud rise up over Denver. Completely freaked out at what she was seeing, but still managing with some part of her mind to execute some form of rational thought, she took the exit for highway 24, steering southward away from Denver.

She opened her window an inch to create an exit draft and lit a cigarette with a shaking hand. Her other hand was gripping the steering wheel tightly. She fought the urge to cry. She was horrified by what she was seeing out her window but was also determined to maintain a façade of normality for Elizabeth's sake.

Her mind flashed on images of mushroom clouds she'd seen in school films - testing on Bikini Island; bombs dropped on Nagasaki and Hiroshima. Other than that, she'd only seen them in movies. She wanted to think that maybe this was some new type of special effect; something that made an image in the sky that didn't really exist. But she knew that was just wishful thinking.

Feeling pretty certain that it was real because it couldn't be anything else, she began to visualize people dying; children playing at school, mothers strolling babies in parks, couples sitting at tables at outside cafes. Her parents! *Oh god, was California hit too?* Her sister in Kansas? Her brother, wherever he was?

She hit the power button on her car stereo and the car filled with the sound of static.

"Mommy. I don't wike this."

She hit the number two preset button and it was the same thing. She hit the other buttons in sequence. Nothing. She hit the power button again, returning the car to relative silence; just the sound of air rushing past her partially opened window.

"Is the music broke, Mommy?"

Tori was even more scared now. She had never even considered the possibility of one day turning on a radio and not hearing something. There were places she'd been where all she could get was country music or Spanish, but there was always something. Tears slowly made their way down her cheeks and her nose started to run.

"Yes, honey. I think the radio's broken." Her voice cracked at the end of the sentence even though she tried so hard not to sound like she was crying. Then she sniffed and wiped her eyes with the back of her hand.

No, dammit. I'm not going to cry. Everything is going to be fine.

"It's okay, Mommy. I'll sing for you."

"Lizzie, you are the sweetest, dearest little person in the whole world. Thank you."

Elizabeth made an exaggeratedly big smile showing all of her teeth and bounced her head from one shoulder to the other, basking in the compliment with delight.

Tori saw her daughter's pigtails flopping around in her rearview mirror and smiled.

"I love you, baby."

"I wuv *you*, Mommy!"

Elizabeth sang the few songs that she knew, over and over until she fell asleep. Tori needed to get her daughter somewhere safe. She didn't know if she had a home anymore, but if she did, going there was not an option. The next thing she thought of was her parent's cabin near Vail. It was far enough from Denver and high enough that it ought to be safe. She would take Liz there and hope there was enough food to last until… she didn't know when. She didn't know what would happen next or if anyone would ever be able to go to Denver again. For now, she just wanted to get someplace safe and get off the highway before another bomb exploded.

Her drive up the mountain was uneventful. There was very little traffic and the weather was clear. Several times she passed cars that had pulled over to the side of the road and she saw the drivers talking and pointing at the mushroom cloud. She was tempted to join them due to an urge to commiserate with other adults and to ask if they knew anything, but she knew that no one could know anything yet.

When she arrived at her parent's cabin, she gently removed Liz from the car-seat and carried her to the front door.

Oh shit.

She did not have a key to the cabin. She couldn't believe she hadn't thought of that - but even if she had, there was nothing she could have done and she would've come here anyway, so she tried to think.

I can break a window. That's my only option.

She carefully deposited Liz on the bench that everyone sat on to remove their snow boots before coming side. She walked around the cabin looking for the best window to break. She circled around and returned to the porch from the opposite side of the cabin and realized that the best window was the one right there in front of the porch.

Once again she mentally chastised herself for being stupid, and then she forgave herself again. How would she know which was the best window for breaking in to her parent's cabin? She had never viewed the windows with that question in mind before. Okay, now she needed to move Liz again.

She put her daughter back in the car-seat, started the engine and left it running to keep the car warm. She found some large stones and brought two of them to the window, and feeling like a vandal, she threw one at the big pane of glass, wincing as it shattered and sounded like the loudest thing she'd ever heard.

She looked around, expecting people to come out of nearby cabins to see what was going on, but no one did. There was a jagged opening at the bottom left side of the big picture window that was nowhere near large enough for a person to fit through. She threw the second stone, aiming higher and to the right this time.

More of the glass broke and fell mostly inside the house. Now she had two holes in the pane and decided she needed to break out an opening manually. The stones had done part of the job but now she needed a stick. A short while later she had an opening she felt she could safely carry Liz through, so she returned to the car to get her and found the car and the car-seat empty.

Four

Carl was dreaming that he was in a bar fight, surrounded by angry women. They threw bottles of whiskey and beer at him, but none of them struck him - his reflexes were too fast. But they were moving in closer. He was going to have to do something more than just duck and swerve to defend himself.

He picked up a pool cue from the table beside him and swung it left and right, testing it and warning the women off. They continued to inch toward him. He swung at the closest woman and felt the reverberation at the base of the cue when it connected with her head. She went down, but the others kept coming, although a little slower now.

Carl was ready for them. In fact, he was eager. It felt good taking one of them out and he looked forward to dropping the rest of them. He grabbed another cue from the table on his left, turned it so that it was vertical and then let it slide through his palm until all but eight inches had passed through, then he gripped it tight. He thought that had to have looked cool.

Now he felt fully prepared for battle. A small, angry brunette rushed him and he swung both sticks toward her head. They both struck at the same time on opposite sides and she dropped to the floor.

Two women broke off from the still slowly advancing group with the intention of flanking him. He whipped his head to the left and to the right, keeping an eye on both of them. He thought, "I can take 'em. I just need to take a piss first."

He raised his hands in the air, looking like he was going to use the pool cues as spears. This was not his intention – he was communicating the wrong thing. He dropped the spears so he could make the correct hand signal and held one hand in the air horizontally while placing the other beneath it vertically.

"Time out! Time out, goddammit. I gotta take a leak."

The women stopped advancing. He looked around for the restrooms, but didn't see any signs. He didn't know this place and he was afraid he wasn't going to be able to find a toilet before he couldn't hold it any longer.

One of the women said, "Why don't you just piss in your pants, asshole?"

He felt like he was going to, the urge was becoming so great. He couldn't stand it anymore, but didn't know where to go. He just kept looking around and willing his bladder to hold on a goddamned second.

Carl opened his eyes and said, "Goddamn. I gotta piss like a motherfucker." He was lying on his back in an empty ski lodge that was the main building in a deserted ski resort, a few miles from the Bunny Resort.

He and Trey had broken in the night before and had sat on the floor drinking beer and smoking pot until they had both passed out. According to the sunlight, they had slept well into the day. They were on private property, but they had no fear of the owner coming to the lodge.

The resort had been vacant for over 40 years and would probably remain vacant forever. The place was fenced off and the owner had posted signs everywhere making it very clear that this was private property. Carl told Trey it would be a great place to crash until they found something better - or until the owner came by and spotted them.

Carl got up quickly then stopped for a second as his head pounded with pain. He put his hand on top of his head and pressed down as if he could stop the pounding sensation that way. He walked to the front door, pulled it open and stepped outside.

He probably would've relieved himself somewhere other than the wooden deck just outside the door if he hadn't had to go so bad, and if his head wasn't still throbbing from a hangover. As it was, he said, "Fuck it," and unzipped right outside the door.

He urinated on the wooden deck, waiting for the urgent, nearly painful feeling to go away. He closed his eyes and concentrated on the relief he'd feel any second. The air outside was cold and felt good at the moment.

Finally, he was past the halfway point of emptying his bladder and he relaxed and felt better. His arms were really feeling the cold air now. He opened his eyes and glanced up to see if it looked like there'd be snow today.

"Holy fucking shit! Trey! Get out here. You gotta see this."

He couldn't believe what he saw on the horizon rising in the sky above the mountains, coming from the Denver area. The unmistakable formation of a mushroom cloud hung in the air. Someone had nuked Denver and Carl thought it was the coolest thing he'd ever seen.

He turned around, zipping up his pants and yelled, "Trey! Wake your ass up, man. You ain't gonna believe this." He squinted his eyes from the pain that yelling brought to his head. "Goddamn, I need a beer."

He walked over to the twelve-pack carton next to Trey and bent down to reach inside one for a can. Again, the pounding pain in his head was there to punish him for the act of bending over. He stood back up with a can of Coors Light, cracked the top and then he kicked the bottom of one of Trey's boots, finally waking him.

"What the fuck, Carl? Why you wanna be a asshole like that?"

"Get up! You gotta see this outside. You'll shit your fuckin' pants."

"Get up so I can shit my pants?"

"No. Grab a fuckin' beer and get your ass out here."

"Fuck. You don't got aspirin, do ya?"

Carl just looked at him for a few seconds, thinking, "Why the fuck would I have a aspirin?"

"What's the big deal? Did you spot a purdy little dear or somethin'?" Trey reluctantly pulled himself up into a sitting position and looked around, rubbing his eyes.

"Come on, dammit! This shit's gonna blow your mind."

"Why don't you tell me what it is, so I got some motivation to get up?"

"What if I told you every single cop in Denver just turned to dust?"

"I'd tell you to share whatever it is you're smokin'."

"I'm serious, Trey. I ain't gonna say anymore. This is somethin' you gotta see for yourself."

Trey's curiosity was finally aroused, although he suspected that Carl had lost his mind or really *was* smoking something that he wasn't sharing. Either way, he wasn't going to find out without getting up and going outside to see what had knocked Carl off his rails. He reached into the twelve-pack case and felt around until his fingers landed on the last can of beer. He grabbed it and got up.

"This better be worth it. A few more hours and I mighta slept past this hangover."

"Trust me, Trey. This is the first day of the rest of our fuckin' lives."

Trey scowled. Carl's statement reminded him of some kind of motivational bullshit he didn't care for. He was wearing a blue denim vest that featured more dirt than blue over a black t-shirt that had faded to dark grey. He reached into the breast pocket for his cigarettes, took one out and lit it with a Bic he found on the floor.

"Okay. Let's see this."

Trey followed Carl out to the deck and looked around, not seeing anything but Carl's big, shit-eating grin.

"Well, I don't see anything. What's this nonsense about cops turning to dust?"

"Ain't that the coolest thing ever?" Carl pointed at the sky over Denver.

Trey looked to where Carl was pointing and his mouth fell open while his eyes widened as far as they could go. He looked panic-stricken.

"No, no, no!"

"Hell, yes, Trey!"

"No, Carl! My fuckin' sister and her kid live down there."

"Not anymore," Carl said.

Trey swung at Carl without thinking, connecting with his jaw and sending the bigger man flying backwards, stumbling and landing on his ass.

"Okay," Carl said, rubbing his jaw. "I'm gonna let you have that one, on account of you just lost family. But try it again, and you'll wish you hadn't."

Trey was ignoring him as he stared at the sky and thought about his kid sister, Tori and her little girl, Lizzy. He realized his parents could also be dead now if bombs had dropped in California too, but that didn't bother him. It was a little sad if his mom was gone, but he never talked to her much anyway since he couldn't stand being around his father. All the bastard ever did was tell him how wrong he was about everything in his life. Fuck him. Good riddance.

Carl got back up and went inside for another beer. The carton was empty. He picked up his keys from the floor and looked around to see if he needed to get anything else before leaving. Finding nothing, he walked back outside.

"Trey, we need to do some shopping."

Trey finally snapped out of his sorrowful trance and his thoughts of what a shame it was for Tori and her cute little kid to have died so young.

"We ain't got any money – 'less you been holdin' out."

"Money? Hell. Who needs money? Don't you know what that big ol' cloud means? Everything's free now. We don't need no money. We *take* what we want. Ain't no fucking cops to stop us." Carl smiled like it was the greatest day of his life.

"Maybe ain't no cops in Denver, but there's still county and state that wouldn'ta been there when the bomb went off."

"Fuck 'em. We'll take them out too. You know why? Cuz there ain't no re-inforcements comin' from Denver! Hooo-weeee!"

Carl walked over to his Harley-Davidson motorcycle, got on it, and put the key in the ignition. "I'm goin' shoppin' anywhere I damn well please. You comin'?"

Carl opted to use the kick-starter instead of the electric starter button. He felt powerful and wanted to exert the energy. Carl revved his engine while Trey went inside to get his keys.

Carl unsnapped the leather knife sheath on his belt and pulled out his hunting knife. He turned it over, looking at one side then the other, and talking to it.

"I think you and me are gonna have to go get us some guns."

He put the knife back and snapped the cover shut and smiled, looking forward to all that life suddenly had to offer him.

Five

Tori panicked and looked all around, desperately hoping to spot the bright pink little ski jacket that Elizabeth wore. She didn't see her anywhere, so she yelled, "Elizabeth! Where are you?!" She walked to the road at the end of the driveway and looked both ways, seeing nothing but trees, widely spaced cabins, and dirty snow.

"Elizabeth!" she called again, not knowing what to do or which way to go to find her daughter. She fought back tears and the urge to panic and tried to think. Where could she have possibly gone? She wasn't walking in either direction down the road - she'd be extremely visible if she was.

She looked around and tried to imagine where would a three-year old go - what would attract her or draw her attention?

"Mommy."

Did she actually hear that, or was she imagining it?

"Where are you, baby? Elizabeth, where are you?"

"I'm right here," the tiny voice sounded from somewhere nearby.

Tori turned to face the cabin and saw the bright pink of her daughter's jacket under her Pontiac Sunbird. She ran the short distance and bent down to reach for her daughter.

"Oh, Jesus, baby. You scared me to death. Why are you under the car?"

"The loud noise was scaring me, so I hided."

"It's okay now, baby. Come here."

Elizabeth crawled to her mother. Tori picked her up and carried her to the porch and set her down for a minute.

"I'm sorry about the scary noise. I had to break this window so we can get inside Grandma and Grandpa's cabin and get warm."

"How come?"

"Because I don't have the key."

"Where's Gramma and Grampa?"

"I don't know, baby."

Tori told herself that she hadn't just lied to her daughter. She didn't *know* that her parents were dead from a nuclear blast, or possibly dying from radiation poisoning. It was just the most probable thing. But she didn't need to tell Elizabeth about what had *probably* happened to her grandparents.

"I'm going to pick you up and carry you through the window. I need you to put your hands in front of your chest and keep them there. We have to be very careful going through the window so we don't get cut. Okay?"

Elizabeth nodded solemnly. Tori picked her up, held her tightly and carefully and slowly ducked and stepped one foot into the front room, crunching glass beneath her foot. She leaned over and gently lowered Elizabeth until her shoes touched the floor.

"You can put your hands down now, but don't move."

Elizabeth stared at the broken glass all over the floor as Tori came through the rest of the way.

"The first thing we have to do is clean up this mess - then we need to cover the broken window. Come with me, baby."

Tori got a broom and dustpan from the utility room near the back door. She left Liz at the dining room table with a coloring book and crayons she took from her little backpack. She cleaned up all of the glass that she could see and feared that there would still be little specks she couldn't see that they'd find with their bare feet. If she ever managed to get the house warm, they would have to wear shoes in the living room. She put the broom and dustpan away and looked for something she could use to cover the window.

She couldn't find anything but sheets and duct tape. Before trying to tape the sheet over the big window, she put a can of soup on the gas stove with a very low flame. She turned around, looked down at Liz and saw that she had drawn a mushroom cloud over a picture of a house with an apple tree in the front yard.

Tori shook her head. She knew that sooner or later Liz would talk about the strange cloud she'd seen and she'd ask Tori if she'd seen it too, and she'd want to talk about it. Tori did not want to tell her daughter about the horror and genocide that had been unleashed on all of the people who lived in their city.

Six

The sound of the two Harleys roaring along the deserted mountain highway bounced off the granite on one side of them then fell away down the cliff on the other. Up here, the air was still clean and the morning was beautiful; like another world, untouched by the nightmare of carnage in the city below.

Carl was driving fast and exploiting the fact that there was little or no chance of being pulled over and hassled for violating the speed limit. He was doing just over 90 mph on turns rated for 45. Trey was also going faster than usual, but was falling further and further behind. He too liked the freedom of being able to drive as fast as he wanted and not worry about having a suspended license or no insurance, but he also wanted to be alive to enjoy this new freedom.

Carl slowed as he reached an intersection. The crossroad was paved to the left for about a quarter mile then turned to gravel as it became a private road with just a few houses. He lit a cigarette and looked at the houses as he waited for Trey to catch up. He could see the cars on the street but the distance was too far to tell if the houses might be occupied or not. It was getting darker, but not dark enough yet for anyone who was home to have any lights on.

He heard the sound of Trey's bike approaching but he was still around a curve and not visible yet. Carl was impatient to check out the houses and see what they could score. If they were lucky, they'd find guns. They needed guns now, and the fact that they were felons and weren't able to legally own them no longer mattered. Carl smiled just thinking about the new order of things.

Trey finally pulled up and stopped his bike. He took out a cigarette and asked Carl what the big smile was about.

"You ever buy a grab bag - where you don't know what you're gonna find inside?"

Trey lit his cigarette and blew out blue smoke that rapidly expanded, whirled around their heads and disappeared with the mountain breeze.

"I know what one is, but I don't know as I actually bought one. Maybe as a kid. Why?"

"That's what I'm looking at down the road. Coupla grab bags. We go in, and who knows what we're gonna find inside?" The big grin was back as Carl felt the thrill and excitement of doing any damned thing he pleased.

"I thought we were going to get beer," Trey replied, not entirely comfortable with just barging into people's houses. The ski resort was okay because it was abandoned, and who cared if you slept in an abandoned place? The owner oughta just donate it to the public anyway as far as Trey was concerned.

"Maybe we'll find some beer inside. Maybe some guns. And if we're really lucky, we might find some women. A couple of hot ones to warm us up. It's cold as a witch's tit out here."

"You can say that again," Trey pretended to agree. He had never understood that expression. Why would a witch have cold tits? A vampire he could understand, but a witch? He wasn't going to tell Carl that he didn't understand it though. No point in making himself look stupid. He'd never heard anyone ask about witch's tits before, and he didn't want to be the first.

Carl took a deep drag off his cigarette and flicked the butt into the road.

"Let's go. Just remember though, we ain't got guns yet and there could be men around. If there is, we gotta play it smart. Just follow my lead. We'll act like we're all shook up about the bomb and such."

Trey nodded in understanding, flicked his cigarette and adjusted his goggles and his scarf, wrapping it back around his ears and neck. Carl took the lead at a moderate speed, as if he was just a guy coming home, or maybe someone who took a wrong turn.

The gravel part of the road was covered with a light layer of snow. Gravel was hard enough to drive a motorcycle on and Carl was not up to the task. His bike went down.

"God damn snow!" Carl yelled. His elbow must've hit a sharp rock when he fell. He felt a stinging pain and blood running down his arm. Trey cruised up next to him at three miles per hour with both feet sliding on the street to keep his bike stable. "Not a word outta you!"

Trey said nothing and waited for Carl to lift his bike up, get back on it and start the engine. Carl copied Trey's slow speed and used his feet the way he saw Trey doing as they slowly approached the six houses.

Two of the houses had cars in their driveways; the first one on the right and the last one on the left. He rolled past the first few and pulled into the driveway of the last house which had a new SUV in the driveway dusted with snow. It had been driven not too long ago. The men got off their bikes and looked around to see if anyone was looking out of their windows or coming outside.

"I'll do the talkin'," Carl said, and started walking up the driveway to the small sidewalk which hadn't been cleared of snow recently. Their boots crunched softly in the few inches of accumulation and left prints that almost revealed the concrete.

Carl pressed the doorbell button as soon as they reached the small covered porch. He looked down at the welcome mat. It was some foo-foo Martha Stewart looking thing. Fucking stupid. At least it meant a woman lived here. No man would buy that shit. And if he did, he wasn't a man.

Carl turned around and looked at Trey who was standing behind him. Trey took a deep breath and blew out twin streams of quickly disappearing vapor from his nose.

"Get ready," Carl said.

Trey nodded, but he didn't look too sure of himself.

Carl slapped Trey's bicep and wiggled his eyebrows. "This is gonna be great. Just wait 'n' see."

Trey looked past Carl as he saw a face appear at eye-level in the small four-pane window set in the upper part of the door. It was a woman. Carl saw Trey's eyes focus on something behind him so he turned around to face the door.

A pretty woman with dark hair was looking through the glass with a questioning look on her face. She wasn't used to getting unexpected visitors.

"Ma'am, did you see what happened?" Carl asked loudly and pointed to a spot in the distance. The woman could not see what he was pointing at and wondered if there was an emergency.

"There's been an explosion and everyone has to head to higher elevation till the authorities clear us to come back down. It may not be safe here, ma'am."

"Who sent you?" the woman asked through the closed door. She was alarmed now, but not pre-disposed to trusting strangers on her porch - especially when they looked like members of a biker gang.

"There aren't enough deputies to talk to everyone, so they deputized us and asked us to help," Carl answered.

"Actually, a deputy pulled over when he saw Carl lose control of his bike." Trey pointed at the fresh blood on the cuff of Carl's sleeve. "He's not hurt too bad so the deputy asked if we could spread the word on the nearby streets that we need to evacuate. He didn't really deputize us. Just asked if we'd help."

Carl glared at Trey for making him out to be a liar and possibly ruining their whole plan

"Ma'am, if you'll check yer phone, you'll find that it's not workin' and that oughta confirm for you that there's trouble on the mountain," Trey added.

The woman raised a hand up to the window, and held up one finger, then quickly walked away.

Carl turned to Trey. "Why'd you tell her that?"

"I figure any lines that go through Denver have to be blown to shit right now. Plus there's that electric magnet shit that fucks up anything that runs on electricity."

Carl didn't know what Trey was talking about, but before he had time to give it any thought, he heard the door open. He turned around and saw the woman standing in her doorway. She was petite with dark brown hair and dressed in expensive casual clothes.

"Where did the Sheriff's deputies say we need to go?" she asked.

"Are your phones out, ma'am?" Trey asked the lady.

"Yes. Both my landline and my cell."

Carl looked at Trey and smiled in admiration. He couldn't believe Trey was actually that smart. He turned back to the woman. "We have to hurry, ma'am. Could you tell everyone inside they gotta get out?"

Trey added, "They said it might be a few hours before we can come back down. Sorry to be the bearers of bad news. I'm sure the sheriff's office will have everything cleared up shortly."

"I'm the only one here. I just need to grab a few things and I'll… where do I need to go?"

That's what Carl was waiting to hear. Once again, Trey's quick thinking paved the way. Boy is smart, Carl thought.

"Well, they said…" Carl rushed the lady like a rodeo bull coming out of the gate. He pushed her backwards into her house until they were well inside. The woman screamed and Carl ordered Trey to shut and lock the door. Carl extended his hands toward her shoulders and shoved hard. The woman lost her footing and fell backwards, landing hard on the carpeted floor.

"Take it easy, man!" Trey urged. His eyes shifted from Carl to the woman and back again. He was frowning in disapproval, and a silent "what the fuck?" burned in his eyes as he stared at Carl, not liking where this was going. Not at all.

Seven

Tori reached the end of *Where the Wild Thing Are,* closed the book and set it down on the bed she and Elizabeth were lying in. Liz was still awake, lying close to her mother and pouting just a little. Tori had gathered all of the blankets she could find. Taping a sheet over the broken window did practically nothing to keep the freezing air outside from coming into the cabin.

The fireplace roared and crackled with a useless fire putting out heat that was obliterated as soon as it entered the room. She remembered a chimney sweep telling her once that 90% of the heat from the fireplace went straight up the flue. A fireplace was more for ambience than anything else. The fire was losing the battle with the icy air flowing through and around the sheet-covered window. Cuddling with Liz under three blankets was warmer than being outside - but just barely.

"What happened to your lip, sweetheart?" Tori asked, looking down at her daughter.

"What yip?"

"That bottom lip of yours - I think it's broken. It's sticking out too far and it makes you look like a sad little girl when you're supposed to be happy."

"I don't want a story, Mommy. I want to watch Burp and Ernie," Liz complained and promptly resumed pouting.

"I know you do, and I've told you we'll watch Sesame Street and Burt and Ernie and Big Bird and everyone else just as soon as the electricity is fixed. But right now, there's nothing I can do about it. Okay, honey?"

Liz's slightly sad face was all she got in response. Tori took a deep breath and then repositioned herself so that she was now lying down under the blankets with Liz. She found Liz's tiny hand and held it in hers.

"If I turn off the light and tell you a mommy story, will you fall asleep?"

"I don't know."

"Let's find out. I'm very tired. I think you are too."

Tori hated to leave the relative warmth of the blankets and her daughter's body heat, but they really did need to sleep. She slid out from under the bedding, keeping the blankets as low to the mattress as she could to prevent the coldest air from getting into the bed and freezing Liz. She ran the short distance to the light switch, flipped it and ran back to the bed. She shivered from the cold air that instantly chilled her flannel pajamas and turned her skin cold.

She knew they couldn't stay here long. It was just too damned cold. She felt a surge of tears as she suddenly became too aware of the fact that she was not taking good care of her daughter right now - holed up in a frozen cabin high in the mountains. But she didn't know what else to do. Where could they go?

By sheer luck, they were alive when so many, many more were not. And by her ability to think somewhat clearly in the face of the most horrific thing she'd ever seen, they now had food and shelter. She felt so fortunate to have just the bare necessities that she almost considered herself selfish over her greedy desire for warmth in addition to what she had.

"Mommy!" Elizabeth pleaded.

Tori cleared her mind of thoughts about gratitude and greed and the steady stream of cold air that would not allow her feet to warm up. She bent her knees and rubbed her feet briskly on the sheet.

"Okay, baby. Let's see... Once upon a time, there was nice mommy who had the most beautiful daughter in all of the land..."

Tori looked down at her daughter and her big grin that came from knowing this was going to be a great story. Liz loved mommy and daughter stories. They were the easiest ones to see when she closed her eyes because all she had to do was pretend that the story was about her mommy and herself.

Eight

Carl spun around and looked at Trey. "You just mind your own," Carl replied with a challenging look. "I'll take care of the lady how I see fit. Why don't you make yourself useful and see if there's any beer. Then check the rooms for guns." Trey dropped his gaze to the floor and went in search of the kitchen, as ordered.

He felt a little disgusted with himself for not standing up to Carl, but what could he do? He owed Carl respect. If it wasn't for Carl, he'd probably be a homeless bum. But as it was, he was in Carl's motorcycle club, and he had even been given his motorcycle by Carl. For the first time he could recall, he had been accepted by people and not made to feel inferior; an outcast. His own family didn't even accept him like the members of the Unforgiven did.

Unforgiven MC - Denver Chapter

He wore their colors with actual pride - and although he wouldn't mention it to anyone in the gang, his self-esteem skyrocketed the day he first wore the denim vest he was given after his successful initiation into the club. It was the first time he didn't feel like the loser his dad always said he was.

He couldn't risk his membership - his new family, by countering Carl. He winced slightly as he heard the woman grunting as she struggled to resist whatever Carl was doing now.

Trey found the kitchen and tried to ignore the sounds coming from the living room. It wasn't his concern, he told himself. He opened the refrigerator and was relieved to see there were plenty of bottles of Coors Light inside. He grabbed two of them and let the door close by itself. Holding a bottle in each hand, he left the kitchen, reversing his path back to the living room where Carl was now straddling the woman's hips and holding one big hand over her mouth. The sound of her voice was muffled, but the high tones of her squealing were still audible.

"I can do this all day, lady. And I will, if you don't get smart and calm the fuck down." Carl was enjoying the hell out of himself on Day One of Anything Goes.

"Gotchu a beer," Trey said from behind him.

Carl turned and took the beer with his free left hand. Trey turned and walked away, heading toward the hallway that led to the bedrooms. Carl's right hand was clamped over the woman's mouth, but now he needed it to twist off the cap because Trey was too stupid to have done it for him.

"I'm gonna give you another chance. When I take my hand away, you'll stay quiet if you're smart. If you're not, you'll see what happens."

Carl lifted his hand and slowly brought it to the top of the beer bottle. The woman stared up at him and eagerly took deep breaths through her mouth, thankful for the increased air she was able to draw in now.

As Carl twisted the cap, the woman bucked as hard she could and let out another war cry, still filled with a fighting spirit and not even thinking of giving up despite being only five feet and one inch tall against Carl's vastly greater size and weight.

She was stronger than Carl thought possible. As she bucked, lifting him up a few inches, his beer spilled onto her shirt. He pushed down on her face with one hand, pinning her head and muffling her screams, and set the beer bottle far off to his left.

"It's time to learn you a lesson." He lifted his right hand and sound of her screaming filled the room for just a second until his left hand came flying in at her face, stopping her voice instantly. Her cheek turned red and both of her lips began to bleed.

She was momentarily dazed. She could feel heat as blood traveled to her cheek to begin immediate repair of broken capillaries. Her mouth felt swollen and numb on the right side. Her brain was rattled and her mind was still for the moment. She continued taking ragged breaths, staring at Carl with a combination of hatred and terror.

Carl took a long swig of the cold beer. It was warm inside the house and his body temperature was high from his increased heartbeat. Taking total possession of this woman was exciting, and he hadn't even gotten started yet. Carl raised his hand as if to strike the woman's face again.

"Do you need another one? I'll be happy to give it to you..."

Her chest rapidly rose and fell with her quick breathing. For the first time, she did more than scream at Carl. Her voice was rough and her throat was dry from adrenaline and exertion.

"My husband will kill you," she told him in barely more than a whisper. "And when he does, you'll go straight to--"

Carl hit her in the face before she could complete the sentence. This time he used his fist. She looked like she was out cold, but just to make sure, he hit her once more. He was tired of playing games with her. She needed to recognize who was in charge of this here situation.

He saw a framed photo of a man in a military uniform sitting on the end table beside the couch. The picture looked like the ones Carl always saw on the freeway, talking about honor, duty and integrity. Shit like that.

"Fuck you, soldier boy. I'm gonna learn your wife what a *real* man is."

He lifted his beer to his mouth and held it there, tipping the bottle further and further up until it was empty. He burped from the large dose of carbon-dioxide and threw the bottle at the framed photograph, shattering both of them. He was just about to pick up the woman and find a place to take her when Trey came back in to the room.

"No beer?" He was starting to think that Trey was less and less useful to have around.

"I'll get you one, but I wanted to show you this. Figured you'd want to know." Trey handed Carl a 3rd generation Glock 17.

Carl's eyes lit up and he smiled.

"This is exactly what I need. Is that all?"

"It's the only thing out in the open. Found it in her closet on the shelf. There's a gun safe in the other room, but I can't open it."

"Find a way," Carl ordered.

"It's one o' them fancy ones with the—"

"I don't give a fuck!" Carl growled. "Find a way in that goddamned safe and get me a beer."

Trey turned to get another beer from the kitchen. He shook his head as he walked.

What the fuck has gotten into Carl? I thought we were friends.

Carl had been fine that morning. Even after Trey hit him, he was still his regular self. Trey thought if he hit Carl now like he did earlier, Carl would probably kill him. He knew Carl was a bad dude, but now it was like he didn't even know him anymore. When Trey returned to the living room with two beers this time, both for Carl, the room was empty.

He went down the hall and checked the master bedroom. He was there. The lady was lying on her bed, still unconscious.

"More beer for you, Carl."

Carl turned around and smiled when saw the bottles.

"You ain't as dumb as you look."

He took both bottles and walked over to the night-stand beside the bed and set one down. He opened the other and took a drink.

"Now get that safe open."

"I'll see what I can come up with," Trey muttered as he walked into the hall, certain that there was no way in hell he could open it.

"And shut the door!" Carl yelled.

Trey came back a few steps and shut the door.

Carl walked over and locked it. He felt a rush of something good start at the base of his skull and then coursing forward and upward to his eyes and forehead. The feeling slowly descended through the rest of his body. It felt like he had just injected something like a speedball - a perfect mix of heroin and cocaine.

He turned back to look at the woman on the bed. He set his beer on her bureau and undressed. As he took his clothes off, his mind filled with images of what he planned to do. He was getting mentally aroused as he envisioned himself raping her, but physically, there was no evidence of his arousal.

He picked up his knife and gun and walked over to the bed. He dropped the gun by her side and watched it bounce once then sink into the down comforter. He opened his knife and carefully cut the woman's shirt most of the way up the middle, being careful not to cut her. He didn't want to hurt her. Not yet. He laughed to himself. Cutting her shirt off with a knife was cool. He'd always wanted to do that. But it was too slow, and he had no patience. He folded the blade back into the handle and dropped it on the floor. He tore her shirt the rest of the way with his hands. The sound of the ripping fabric started to arouse him.

Trey stood staring at the safe. The only thing he could think of was to try finding a drill. But if he could find one, he didn't know where exactly he should make a hole. He had no understanding of the mechanics of safes, but in movies, they always drilled holes, so if he did that, at least he could tell Carl he was trying.

After finding a drill in the garage and trying it on the front and sides of the safe with nothing to show for it but a broken drill bit, Trey was ready to give up. He sat on the bed that was made up for guests and tried to think.

A few minutes later, still with no ideas, he began to hear the woman's muffled cries coming from the other room. Carl must've gagged her with something. It sounded like she was crying into a pillow. It also sounded like she was in pain. Trey couldn't stand hearing it.

This was so fucked up, he thought. He could hear the headboard hitting against the wall with a rhythmic thumping. Carl was raping the lady. Perfect. This was not what he had in mind when he thought about there being no law enforcement. Yeah, they were outlaws, and they stole from people who had more than enough, but no one in the club ever raped anyone.

It occurred to Trey that maybe he wouldn't lose the respect of his peers if he intervened on the lady's behalf. It was a bold thought, but what if the guys actually agreed with Trey and praised him for saving her? Hell, all of them had girlfriends, so they should be able to relate to how it would feel if someone did to them what Carl was doing right now.

Yeah. He was certain they'd approve. Maybe they'd even kick Carl out of his own club - because he'd lost his fucking mind. Skull would probably take over. He was more of a leader anyway, and a lot smarter than Carl was.

The thumping noise was louder now and the woman's muffled screams were keeping time with the thumps. That was it. Trey made up his mind. He was putting a stop to this shit. Right fucking now.

He got up and quickly lit a cigarette with trembling fingers. He clenched his teeth and focused his anger and outrage and summoned up his courage and resolve. He walked out of the room, went several steps over to the other room where the door was shut. He grabbed the doorknob and tried to twist it.

He pounded on the door.

"That's enough, Carl! I'm calling you out!" Trey didn't know why he'd said that, but he'd heard it in a western once before a gunfight, so it seemed like a good thing to say.

Carl was thrusting into the woman from behind in a doggy-style position. He had secured her hands behind her back with his belt. Since she couldn't support herself, she was face down in the pillow. Carl was holding her up with his hands gripping her hips. He tried to think of something to say in response to Trey's annoying interruption, but he couldn't think of anything. He was already having trouble maintaining his erection and was concentrating hard on fucking. He couldn't just switch mental gears and come up with a good reply that would put Trey in his place.

"Just fuck off now!" he yelled over his shoulder toward the door.

"Stop it, Carl, or I'm busting in and stopping you. We ain't like this. The Unforgiven don't do rape. I think everyone will back me on this."

Carl's brain lit up with anger at Trey's defiance and mention of the club backing him and turning on Carl. He chose not to respond and felt his anger translate itself into increased blood flow where he needed it most. Finally, he was getting hard. He started ramming himself into the woman harder than before.

"Count of three, Carl!

Carl looked at the bed to see where his gun had gone. The blanket was all bunched up and probably covering the gun somewhere. Goddamn Trey. Carl didn't mind having it out with him, but he'd prefer if it could wait till he was finished.

"One!"

Carl felt his body preparing to climax. This was the worst time to have to stop and find the damned gun. Trey was going to be very sorry he had fucked with him. He slapped the woman's ass and said, "I'll finish with you in a second."

Trey was about to yell out, "Two!" when he realized this wasn't going to be easy and he'd have a badly needed advantage if Carl didn't know right when to expect him. Why was he counting and giving him advance notice? Trey stepped back as far as he could and then charged the door with his shoulder out front.

Carl was moving the blanket around, looking for his gun before Trey reached "three." He flapped the blanket and the Glock flew off the bed and landed on the floor. He turned to retrieve it and heard the wood crack and splinter as Trey busted into the room and kept on coming until he slammed Carl in the back, sending him flying forward and slamming his head on the corner of the nightstand beside the bed. Carl went down and moaned, slowly bringing one hand up to his bleeding head.

Trey rushed over to Carl before he could start to recover and kicked him once in the face with his heavy, steel-toed boot. Trey was scared at what he had just done, but what choice did he have? Even if the rest of the guys didn't back him, he had to do it. He wasn't a fucking monster.

He went to the woman and fumbled with the belt, trying to unbuckle it with his trembling hands. He constantly looked from the belt to Carl to see if he was going to get up. With the belt undone, he picked up the gun and tucked it into his waistband.

"Ma'am, I am so sorry about this. I didn't know. I really didn't know. I hope you believe me." He looked at her swollen eyes with the flesh around them turning purple, and the blood around her mouth that had dripped down to her chin. "This is bad. I'm so sorry!"

The woman immediately rolled over onto her back when he she felt the belt fall away from her hands and she rapidly scooted backwards away from Trey until she reached the headboard. She had pulled the blanket along with her and held it up over her body as she went, staring wild-eyed at Trey. He felt like he was in a horror movie and didn't know if he was a good guy or a bad guy. He had helped make this possible.

"You're safe now. I swear to God I'm not going to hurt you. But we need to get out of here. He'll kill us both if he gets a chance." He needed her to believe him, but she just stared at him like she was in shock. She pulled her knees up to her chest with the blanket bunched up in front of her and she shook like she was having a mild seizure. Trey couldn't tell if she understood him or was even hearing his voice. This was the most awful thing he'd ever seen.

It was pretty clear to him that she wasn't going to be any help getting them out of there. He looked at Carl and although he still appeared to be in no danger of waking up any time soon, Trey didn't want to take any chances so he kicked his head again, then turned and ran to the kitchen where he remembered seeing the woman's purse.

Trey unsnapped the purse and was relieved to see that her keys were inside. He also saw a small I.D./credit card holder and looked at the woman's name. Monica Lourenz. He dropped the I.D. back into the purse and took it with him as he ran back to her room. Carl was still down and out. He went to her closet and grabbed a travel-case and laid it on the end of the bed.

"You're going to be okay, Monica. I'm gonna to get you some clothes and get you outta here. I wish you'd help me though. And it'd be good if you could put on some clothes."

Monica's breath began to hitch and she moaned like a wounded animal at the sound of Trey's voice. He grabbed clothes at random from her bureau and threw them into the case. He figured he had enough now and ran out to her SUV with the case in one hand and her keys in the other. He threw the case in the back and started the engine, then ran back inside.

He looked at Carl as soon as he entered the room. Still safe. "Monica, my name is Trey. I need you to trust I'm not gonna hurt you. I just want to take you someplace safe, okay?"

She looked up at him with what could have been a look of terror laced with hope that he was telling the truth. Trey's heart was ripping him up inside and he hated himself for having had any part in this. His one hope was that she was actually listening to him now and believing him. Maybe she was coming out of shock and would trust that he wouldn't hurt her.

"If you don't get dressed really fast, I'm gonna have to carry you out to your truck like you are. We really gotta go. I'll turn around if you'll get up and put some clothes on."

She made no move to do anything or go anywhere. Trey approached her slowly with his hands extended out to his sides, palms up. "I'm going to carry you now. Okay, Monica? Don't be scared. You're safe now."

Monica continued to stare at Trey as he approached her. She kept looking at him with that look of hope and fear, but she didn't try to get away as he reached for her. She just looked at him and her teeth began chattering as if she were freezing. Trey reached behind her with one hand and under her with the other, scooping her up off the bed. He struggled to get the blanket wrapped around her while holding her up with his knee.

He carried her to the door and adjusted her weight so he could turn the doorknob. He carried her out to her vehicle, leaving the door open behind him. *Dammit,* he thought. *I should have left the car door open, but I wanted it to be warm inside.* He managed to open the passenger door with the hand he had around her back.

He placed her on the passenger seat and fastened her seat-belt. The blanket fell away from her and she pulled it back up, covering herself again. Trey ran around to the other side, got in and slowly backed out of the driveway, fearing that any second Carl would come running out and either shoot them, or maybe he'd just grab the vehicle and stop it as he broke the windows and pulled them out through the broken glass like some kind of insane killer from a horror movie where the bad guy keeps coming back and never dies.

"I'm taking you somewhere safe till we can find your husband. My family has a cabin nearby."

"Thank you," Monica whispered and began to cry.

Nine

Tori stopped the story when she heard Elizabeth's breathing become shallow and even. She looked down at her little girl and made a silent promise to find them someplace warm tomorrow. Or she'd find a way to insulate the broken window. There had to be something. It was ridiculous that they were freezing to death inside of a house.

She turned onto her side and laid as close to Liz as she could and put her arm around her, willing her body heat to transfer into her daughter. Her teeth started to chatter and she was thankful that Liz was asleep and therefore a little warmer than her and unaware of how cold it was in the room.

Tori thought about how much different her life was just one day ago. She almost laughed when it occurred to her that she no longer had a job. The reason she no longer had a job wasn't funny, but the way her whole life changed in an instant, how her whole world had changed today, it made her concerns of yesterday utterly ridiculous.

A few hours before she had left Kelly's house to head back to Denver, Kelly tried as she always did to talk Tori into moving to Kansas. They were sisters, she said. They needed to be closer and see each other more often, and she wanted to be a bigger part of Elizabeth's life.

Tori agreed with Kelly's points, but she really liked Denver and she *didn't* like Salinas. She couldn't imagine living there. Her sister would be the only good thing in her life if she moved there. And she'd have to start over from scratch looking for a job. Just that alone was a depressing thought. She liked her current job. Well, the job she had up until yesterday, she reminded herself.

Tori worked as a CNA at a retirement center in Westminster and had just gotten approval for partial company financing to go to school to become an R.N. The future was just starting to look brighter for her. She wouldn't be forever worrying about how she was going to provide for Elizabeth. Yesterday she was stressed about the time she would have to spend away from Liz while going to classes, which they would both hate, but she finally convinced herself it would be worth it. She had agonized for months over whether she should go to school or not. While she was grappling with the ironic merits of not being there for her daughter in order to be a better mother, her sister was relentlessly urging her to move to Salinas.

Liz rolled over in her sleep and faced Tori. Tori tucked the blankets under Liz's far side and adjusted the trim so it was just below Liz's chin. She softly stroked her daughter's hair as she gazed at her sleeping little angel face.

As frustrating as it was having to constantly convince Kelly that she and Liz were happy in Denver and wanted to stay in Denver - she now had to give her sister credit for her and Liz being alive. If they hadn't gone to Kelly's for a visit, they'd be dead now - like everyone else.

Tori hoped it was only Denver that got destroyed. It was bad enough that she most likely lost her parents today; she didn't want to think about the possibility that Kelly might be dead too. She had no idea where her brother was. He might be nothing but ash billowing around on the streets downtown, or he could be somewhere up here on the mountain with the biker gang he'd been hanging out with lately.

Tori rubbed her feet together, hoping that if she made enough friction, she might be able to at least feel them again. Her eyes flew open. Her feet were numb! She reached under the blanket and felt Elizabeth's feet. They were icy cold.

"Oh God. I have to pull my head out of my ass."

She had thought she could just address the problem of the window in the morning. *Right.* She wanted to be a nurse, and here she was sitting around waiting for herself and her daughter to succumb to frostbite. She berated herself silently for being so stupid and putting both of them in such grave danger.

She got out from under the blankets and sat up, determined to do something about the window *right now.* This wasn't something to be dealt with later. They were freezing in here. They could die of frostbite. Jesus. What had she been thinking?

She doubled her half of the blankets over Liz, effectively putting her under six layers of bedding. Her hands hurt from the cold. She started to rub them together to warm them up, and that made them hurt more. She stopped and told herself to think. What did she know about frostbite? She needed to warm them with heat. She put her hands under her armpits and held them there. Then she tapped her right foot on the ground. She still had sensation in her heel. Good. She'd be able to walk to the kitchen without damaging the flesh on the bottom of her feet.

She fought against the pain in her hands as she put her shoes on, and then walked on her heels through the cabin and into the kitchen. The area near the broken window was no longer the coldest spot in the house. It was that cold everywhere now. The inside temperature was close to equalizing with the outside temperature.

In the kitchen, she turned on the sink and was relieved that the pipes hadn't frozen. She filled a big pot with water, lit all four of the gas burners with an igniter sitting on the counter and set the pot on the burner one nearest her.

She held her hands high above the flames to the left of the pot of water. She resisted the urge to hold her hands closer where she would feel the heat more intensely. She knew that the warmth would feel so good that she'd end up burning her hands. As she waited for the water to warm up, she lifted her feet, one after another, walking in place on her heels to try to get her blood circulating and spreading what little warmth she had inside of her around her body.

She looked around the kitchen and then walked into the living room and took the three cushions off of the couch and brought them back to the kitchen, placing them on the floor between the stove and the table, end to end. Then she went and got Liz and carried her into the kitchen and laid her down on the cushions.

"Shhhh. Go back to sleep, baby," she whispered as Liz stirred while being laid down on the makeshift bed.

Tori looked at the water and saw small bubbles forming on the bottom of pot. She lifted it carefully and put it on the floor, then sat down on one of the dining chairs and removed her shoes and socks. She tested the water with a finger. It was hot, but not too much so. She slowly lowered one foot into the pot and waited for the water to warm her freezing foot. As the blood warmed and her circulation resumed, she grimaced at the pain and resisted the instinct to remove her foot. The pain was a good thing. Her foot was coming back to life.

After she could fully feel her feet and the pain subsided, she put her socks and shoes back on. Then she had an idea she couldn't believe she hadn't thought of sooner. She went to the bedroom and stripped the sheet off the mattress. She lifted the mattress off the box-spring and hefted it up on its side. Keeping it balanced with her hands, she walked over to the end closest to the door and then walking backwards, she pulled the mattress toward the living room.

After bringing it through the doorway, she stood it up on its end length-wise and with her arms stretched out holding it by the sides, she walked it forward, pushing it with her body until she had it in front of the window. She pulled the bottom of the mattress back toward her, causing the top half to learn forward and fall against the window which it more than covered completely. Then she pushed the couch from the adjacent wall, first from one corner, then the other, until she had it in front of the mattress. She shoved the couch forward, pinning the mattress in place.

She smiled at her handiwork and waited a minute to catch her breath. She smiled as she felt the heat from the fireplace already start to warm her arms.

Ten

When Carl woke up, his head was killing him. It took a few seconds for him to figure out where he was and then to remember what the hell had happened. That fucking Trey! He was going to die. Carl got up and his head throbbed far worse than it had this morning. The pain was all over the place and it was sharp and throbbing.

He brought a hand to his face and felt the sticky blood drying on his skin. He carefully felt around his head and found three different large bumps.

"That mother-fucker."

A slow burning rage was building inside of Carl.

He got up carefully. He looked around the room and saw that Trey must've taken the woman for himself. That's alright, he thought. He'd get her back. Carl found his clothes and dressed slowly. His head was killing him and every movement made it worse.

He decided he needed rest. He dropped the boot he was about to put on and slowly lay backward onto the bed. He didn't have to rush out right now in god-awful pain to go get his revenge on Trey and re-claim his woman. He had time. He was sure he'd have no problem finding him. There was really only one place he could be headed.

Trey's parents had a cabin not too far from here. It would be empty and the most obvious place for the dumbass to go. Carl closed his eyes and thought about what he'd do to Trey when he found him. Trey was going to regret what he'd done. He had a hell of a lesson comin' to him.

Carl would not tolerate being disrespected like this.

"It ain't what you don't know that gets you into trouble. It's what you know for sure that just ain't so." – Mark Twain

Part 3

Comin' Down Fast

Chapter One

Trey knew he had hurt Carl but he didn't know how badly, so he had no idea how much time he had to get himself and Monica out of Carl's reach. At the intersection where Monica's street reached the highway, he turned hard to the right causing the minivan to slide around the corner. With adrenaline feeding his body and brain, he expertly corrected and rapidly accelerated.

Monica stared straight ahead, seemingly unconcerned by the vehicle sliding on every sharp curve of the snow-slicked road. Trey knew he was driving too fast, but he didn't feel he had a choice. He just needed to be careful and get to a safe place. His eyes frequently left the road as he searched for a place to pull over to see if he could get Monica into some clothes. He was fairly certain they wouldn't run into any law enforcement, but if they did, he didn't want to be in a position of having to explain why he was traveling with a nude woman who was in shock with a bloody and bruised face.

No, I didn't beat her and rape her, officer – a friend of mine did that.

His mind focused on three priorities, in order: Get away from Carl, get Monica dressed, and get to safety. The snowfall began to increase and Trey looked at the unfamiliar controls on the steering column. He grabbed the one on the left and turned it like accelerating a motorcycle in reverse. The windshield wipers came on at full speed. The rapid swiping motion made him feel nervous, as if the car was panicking and causing him to feel panicky too. He rotated the control back toward himself and the wipers slowed to a less frantic pace.

The sky was a large expanse of blended grey and white. He spotted a small black stream of wispy smoke flowing upward from a house somewhere off to his right. Someone had just started a fire, or had just let one go out in their fireplace or woodstove. Maybe they would help. The turnoff toward the house was coming up immediately on his right. He braked too hard as he made the turn. The minivan spun around and did a 360 while sliding forward at an angle.

The front end slammed into a utility pole, breaking the windshield and bringing the van to a complete stop, catapulting Trey through the windshield. He flew through the air and hit a stone retaining wall bordering a large front yard. Monica jerked forward but was restrained by her seatbelt. She clawed at the airbag covering her face. She coughed from the cornstarch released from the deployment. The driver side airbag was draped over the van's short hood, flapping in the breeze. After the loud crunching sound of the collision, and the airbags deploying, there was silence except for a hissing sound from under the hood.

Monica's eyes were more alert and active now than they had been since Trey carried her out of her house. She brought her trembling hands to her face and cried. Freezing cold air blew into the van and she became more aware of her absence of clothing. She looked down at the blanket wrapped around her as if she didn't remember how or why that was all she had covering her flesh. She desperately wanted some clothes to wear and to get warm.

She looked over at the empty driver's seat. She knew the van had been in a collision but didn't remember Trey getting out. Her mind was only beginning to work regularly as she came out of shock so she dismissed the mystery of where Trey had gone and resolved to get dressed somehow. She turned around in her seat and saw one of her suitcases in the cargo area. She looked out the window to her right at the empty and silent street, then dropped the blanket and quickly squeezed herself between the bucket seats, then scrambled over the second row of seats and released the hasps on her suitcase.

She didn't know who had packed her clothes or why they were packed so badly, but she was glad to have them. As she got dressed, she noticed bruises on her arms and legs. An image flashed into her mind of a large and violent psychopath. She immediately pushed the thought away. She did not want to think about what had happened to her. Not now; maybe not ever.

Now that she was dressed, she looked around for shoes and didn't see any. Apparently, whoever had packed her case didn't think she'd be going outside. She needed to go… she almost thought the word "home," but stopped herself. She needed to go *somewhere*. She couldn't sit here freezing to death in her wrecked minivan.

Two

Carl awoke the next morning feeling like someone had dropped a load of bricks on his head. This angered him because he was certain that if he had gotten enough sleep he'd wake up feeling better. But he felt worse. He raised one arm and carefully checked the several bumps on his head. They were no smaller than before he had slept. He clenched his teeth and squinted his eyes nearly shut thinking of Trey and the payback he had coming to him.

He slowly got out of Monica's bed and looked in her closet. Nothing but women's clothes. Alright then, where did her damned husband sleep? Were things not going so well between the army boy and his pretty little lady? Carl wasn't surprised. She was a hellcat. Probably didn't know her place with her old man either.

He left the room to check the one across the hall. Here was the safe that Trey had tried and failed to break into. Carl yearned to open the safe. He imagined it being filled with shiny, new weapons. Trey had taken the Glock and left him with nothing. He wished he had some dynamite. He'd blow the thing wide open, right there in the goddamned bedroom.

Further down the hall he found one more door. He opened it and saw the inside of a two car garage. He flipped on the light switch next to the doorway and looked around. Aha! A stack of clothes on a workbench, all wrapped in dry cleaning bags. Carl walked over to the stack of clothing and cycled through each item, extracting the few things that he found least objectionable.

Included with the dress pants, dress shirts and military uniforms were also khakis and flannel shirts. Finally on the bottom of the stack he found the sole pair of Levi's and added them to his small collection.

"What kinda man dry-cleans his Levi's?" Carl grumbled, shaking his head. He went back inside, found the bathroom and showered, carefully washing the blood from his face and head, trying to not re-open the wounds. After toweling off, he put on the Levi's which just barely fit. They were uncomfortable but would have to do for now. There was no deodorant or men's shaving cream; not even a man's razor among all of the women's stuff in the cabinet above the bathroom sink.

"Fuck it," Carl said to himself. Real men didn't need any of that shit anyway. It was fine with him if he looked and smelled like a man. Besides, he'd like to see the man or woman with the balls to say anything. He went to the bedroom and as he was putting on his dirty socks and his boots, hunger suddenly struck him like a freight train slamming into his stomach. He wrapped his arms around his stomach and doubled over from the sudden pain. He hadn't eaten since the day before yesterday.

"God damn!" he said, straightening up. "I gotta eat somethin'."

He went to the kitchen and scowled at how nice and pretty everything was with perfect little curtains that decorated a window next to the dining table with a view to the backyard. Placemats in four places at the table with some kind of wheat pattern on them. A white tablecloth with fall leaves scattered about sparsely. Carl kicked the edge of the table, sending it sliding into the corner.

He turned and walked the few steps to the refrigerator. He opened the door and couldn't believe the lack of food that he found on the shelves. Some Coors Light and a couple of yogurt containers on the top shelf next to some almond milk.

"How the fuck do you get milk out of an almond for Christ's sake?"

In the door there were two rows of eggs. Carl took one out on the chance that they might be hard-boiled. He threw it into the sink hoping for a dull thud but it splattered and leaked yolk. He opened a drawer labeled Meat and found a package of Uncured Bacon. He didn't know what that meant, but bacon was bacon as far as he was concerned. He'd even eat some of that fake-ass turkey bacon if that was all he could find.

After a breakfast of bacon and scrambled eggs with almond milk, Carl felt a lot better, but still hungry. He decided he'd had enough from this kitchen though. He'd get some real food like a big-ass steak from somewhere else. The diner down the mountain should be a goldmine of food, and everything would be free.

He found his jacket and his gloves and went back to Monica's room to get the stuff out of his pants pockets. Now that he had bathed and eaten, he was aware of the stench coming from his grimy Levi's. He almost wanted to wash his hands after handling them.

He went outside and started up his bike. He looked at Trey's bike and thought about setting it on fire but remembered it was actually his. He had given it to the back--stabbing bastard. He'd figure out a way to come back for it later. He looked at the driveway while he let his engine warm up. He saw a large rectangular area in the center of the driveway with less snow than the surrounding area. There were no tire tracks visible from when the van had driven away. That was okay. He knew where to find them.

He brushed his left foot back to raise the kickstand and he revved the engine a few times. He started off slowly, releasing the clutch and giving the bike only a little gas but he still laid it down as he turned out of the driveway and onto the gravel.

He got up cursing and kicking at his bike. He strained to lift it and got it upright. He put the kickstand back down and looked around. He needed four wheels in this shit. He didn't know how to hot-wire, so he needed keys. That meant he needed to find a car where the owner was at home. He looked at the house across the street. He couldn't tell if anyone was home or not. The porch light was off and there was no car in the driveway, but that meant nothing since most folks would have their cars inside their garages when it snowed.

He walked across the street and pounded on the door. An old man with wispy white hair decorating his mostly bald head came to the door wearing a thick green robe. The man pushed a small curtain aside from the window in the door and looked at Carl with interest.

"Yes?" he asked loudly, without opening the door.

Carl was wearing normal clean clothes, but his face was bruised and unshaved so he knew he didn't look like the nicest of strangers to be appearing at someone's door. He thought quickly.

"Excuse me, sir. I'm trying to get home to Edwards and my little girl don't think she can hold it that long. Could you be so kind to let her use your bathroom real quick? Her momma died last week and I just hate making her suffer more than she already is. She cried all night."

The old man had concern in his eyes as he listened to Carl's plea. He unlocked the door and as soon as he started to open it Carl kicked it with the bottom of his boot, putting all of his lower-body strength in to it. The old man was flung inward with the door and slammed into the wall. He crumpled to the ground, his body pushing the door slowly back toward Carl who stuck his arm out to stop it, then let himself inside.

"Anybody home?" he yelled. Probably no one else there except for maybe an old woman, but he wanted to make sure. No one responded so Carl cautiously made his way further into the house. The place *sounded* empty, he thought, but someone could be sleeping. He went down the hall and looked in the bedrooms. The floor plan was the same as Monica's. The master bedroom had an empty unmade bed. The second room looked like an office with a leather couch and lots of bookshelves filled with more books than Carl had ever seen outside of a library. He shook his head at the absurdity of one person having so many books. People were fucking strange. He opened the last door that he knew would lead to the garage.

"Now *that's* what I'm talkin' about!" he said as he flipped on the light switch causing bright fluorescent light to illuminate a 1932 Ford Roadster gleaming on the clean concrete floor like it had just rolled off the production line. The deep red paint was so glossy it looked wet. The top was off and Carl walked over and looked inside to see if the keys were in it. They weren't.

He went back into the house. He was excited about the car. If he could score a firearm or two, he'd leave here in style, ready to take on the world. If only his head wasn't still throbbing. Carl found a keychain on a hook in the dining room but he did not find any guns other than a civil war musket hanging on the wall above the fireplace.

He grabbed a banana from a fruit bowl on the table and went to the garage. He tried to open the garage door from inside, but it was locked. The key to the padlock was on the keychain. He entered the garage from the driveway and got into the roadster. Now he just needed this thing to start. He hoped to hell that it wasn't just a museum piece. He turned the key and the sound of the engine revving to life made him smile. He backed out into the street then shifted into Drive.

He wanted to see what the V8 under the hood could do, so he floored the gas, expecting to peel out, thinking of how cool he'd look burning rubber in a fancy hot rod, but the wheels just spun on the wet rocks, sending gravel flying up into the under-carriage and the street behind him. Disappointed, he let up on the gas and drove slowly to the end of the street, turning left onto the paved road which was coated with a thin layer of slushy snow.

As he drove down the mountain, he wondered if he should go back and look for the convertible top, but he decided to stick with his forward momentum and just keep going. The wind was cold and wet snow blew around him and stuck to the windshield, but he was too excited to care. It even seemed like his head hurt less - at first.

Three

Angela hated the windows being boarded up so she wanted to get out of the lodge and go sit in one of the cabins. Things were bad enough for her with the possible nuclear war, her friends dying, being stuck on the mountain and unable to go home, and now, sitting around in a boarded up building with hardly any sunlight - it was just too much. She was trying to stay as positive as she could under the most negative of circumstances. But it was hard. And now the dreary darkness of the lodge just made it feel impossible.

After Terry explained why he'd boarded up the windows and they talked about staying together to survive as a group if they couldn't resume their normal lives, she left the men to sort through and separate the loot from their last scavenging run, saying, "I'll be back later," and started walking toward the door. "Oh, could somebody cook something for tonight? I'm really tired and just want to rest a while."

"Sure. I will," Terry replied.

Both men watched Angela leave, then Terry looked at Jim.

"Is she okay? She seems sort of depressed."

Jim shrugged. "Don't know. Probably that whole nuclear bomb thing, followed by watching her best friend die in the parking lot."

Terry shook his head and resumed sorting supplies from the big pile.

"You *do* care about her, don't you?"

Jim looked at Terry and bit the inside of his cheek. He reached for a knife and dropped it with several others off to the side. Then he examined the pile to see what he could sort next. He started on medical supplies. After he gathered them into a separate pile, he stood up and stretched. Terry was picking up ammo and sorting it by caliber.

"I'm gonna grab some empty boxes," Jim said, walking toward the front door.

Terry thought that was a bad lie since the empty boxes were in the back by the pantry, but he didn't say anything.

Jim stepped outside and stood still after taking a few steps away from the door. He looked over at the cabins and saw the light on in Angela's. Her curtains were closed. A cold wind blew through his shirt but he didn't button his jacket. He just stood there, staring at the one cabin with a lit window. He put his hands in his jacket pockets, tilted his head down and began walking toward the light.

When he reached her door, he tapped it with the side of his shoe three times. A few seconds later, the door opened and he could see Angela's breath inside the room as easily as he could see his outside.

"You're gonna freeze in there. You should come back to the lodge."

She turned around and went back to sitting on the bed. She picked up several long strands of grass and started braiding them together. Jim came in and shut the door.

"You makin' a wreath?"

She nodded. He sat down in the upholstered chair to the left of the bed. He kept his hands in his pockets, trying to keep them warm.

"What's up, Ange?"

She stopped fiddling with the grass and looked at him without turning her head.

"What do you mean?" She looked down at her hands but kept them still.

"You seem off. I know life is sucking pretty hard lately, but you seem different tonight. Is something wrong, aside from the world coming to an end?"

She snorted and mildly shook her head, still looking down at the grass she was holding. She started fiddling with it; not braiding it as she was before, but just rolling strands between her fingertips.

"It's hard, Jim. We still don't have any clue about what's going. I think part of why I've been able to block out the horror of what happened to Denver is because I can hope that it only happened there and that our family and friends at home are still okay. But I don't even know. Everyone we care about could be dead."

"Yeah, but that wasn't bothering you earlier today, or yesterday. What changed?"

She turned her head to look at him. She rolled her lips inward and inhaled deeply through her nose. Her exhalation was a long sigh.

"You'll think it's stupid."

Jim bit the inside of his cheek and waited.

"I know this doesn't make any sense, so please, don't tell me how stupid I am, okay? It's just… I think it's the windows being all boarded up. I hate it."

"You don't have any matches, do you?"

"No."

Jim took his hands out of his pockets and cracked his knuckles by interlacing his fingers and extending them away from his body.

"Why do the boarded up windows bother you so much?"

"I'm not sure. I just know that's when I felt different - right after we got back from stealing people's stuff." She looked at him, waiting to see if he was going to correct her again on the difference between stealing and scavenging. He didn't, so she continued.

"The lodge looks condemned, you know? It was a lot easier to not think about how awful things were while we were sitting on a beautiful mountain top, at a ski resort, which is a great place to be in general. It's a place for fun, vacation, getting away from it all, and so on. When you're sitting by the fireplace, listening to the wood crackle and pop, looking out the window at the snow falling - you can just - I don't know, not think about the reality of the situation.

"But now It's like we're living in a building that has been officially condemned; designated unsafe by a city inspector or something. Like it's going to be torn down. No more lodge. No more skiing. No longer a place where people go to have fun. It changes everything here. And now all I can think about is how it's just like our lives. They're shut down; condemned; not fun anymore." She looked at him for a moment. "Things are really fucked up, Jim."

Angela tore the grass she was holding in half and started to cry. Jim got up at once and sat beside her, putting his arm around her. She turned toward him and put her arms around his back and laid her head on his shoulder, muffling her cries in his jacket.

Jim bit his lip as he held her and stared at the wall on the other side of the room. He had a million things he wanted to say to her, but he said nothing. He reached up with one hand and softly stroked her hair. Angela was surprised to feel Jim doing something so gentle and affectionate. She lifted her head up and moved back a few inches so she could see his eyes.

"Now that I told you my stupid feelings about the boarded up windows, maybe I should tell you my other stupid feelings."

"Ange, you can tell me anything you want and I'll never think you're stupid." He understood what she had said about the lodge looking and feeling condemned now. He didn't like it either, but if it made them safer, he was in favor of it.

Angela moved her hands up from Jim's back and locked her fingers together behind his neck. She took a deep breath. She never thought she would ever say what she was about to say. There had never been any point in it before. She had always liked Jim romantically but he had never shown any interest in her, so she just acknowledged that she had feelings for him, and that her feelings didn't matter. They weren't something to get worked up over.

But for the time being, there weren't any other people around. And the population in general might be drastically reduced for all they knew. Now her feelings for Jim had become much more significant to her, and she thought that under the circumstances he might have started to feel something for her too.

"Jim, I really like you a lot, and I have for a long time. I'm sure you know that. I've been wondering if… God, now I feel stupider than ever, so I'm just going to spit it out. I want to be with you, Jim. Do you feel anything like that for me?"

Before he could respond she quickly moved in and kissed him. It was the first time they had ever kissed and it was just how she imagined it would be. He was such a cold and hard person, inside and out, but his lips were so soft and warm, just like hers. She took his bottom lip between both of hers and relished the feeling. She had wanted to kiss him for so long. A desire she'd tried to ignore for years awoke inside of her and she felt her dark depression start to fade away.

When she felt Jim kissing her back, she took that as the answer to her question about whether he had feelings for her or not. He wanted her too. Despite everything that was happening in the world, she rejoiced in the knowledge that there could still be love. She wrapped her arms around him tightly and parted his lips with her tongue. Years of pent up desire for Jim was suddenly unleashed and she wanted to kiss him without ever stopping.

Jim drew back from her and gently put his hands on her shoulders.

"Angela..."

She smiled, gazing into his eyes. She couldn't believe it. The look on his face was so serious. Did he actually love her? Jim, who hated just about everyone, was going to say, "I love you?" She couldn't wait to hear the words.

"Yes?"

"I could never be with you."

She froze. The cold air in the room went right through her clothes, through her skin and into her bones. She felt like her heart stopped beating and her blood stopped flowing. Her ears burned and her throat closed tight around a lump that suddenly grew and made it impossible for her to swallow. She thought she was going to choke on the lump if she didn't vomit from the queasy sickness that was now roiling in her stomach and rising upward.

She finally breathed. It was a sobbing gasp of air that hurt as it went in. She pulled her hands away from him as if he was toxic and she moved away from the bed and looked around the room frantically as if she was going to panic. She had never felt more stupid in her life. A flood of tears gushed from her eyes as she ran from the room, leaving the door open behind her. She cried out loudly as she ran. She couldn't hold back the pain. She didn't care if he heard her crying. She didn't know how she could ever face him again anyway.

"Angela, wait! Come back!" The sound of her crying diminished as she got further away. She wasn't coming back. "Angela!" he yelled, getting up to run after her.

She was running across the parking lot. Jim ran toward her. She was reaching for the door handle of the BMW when he caught up to her.

"You can't leave. Where do you think you're going?"

"Anywhere away from here," she said, opening the car door and sliding inside. Jim ran around to the other side and got in quickly before she could lock the doors.

"Angela, you don't understand..."

"I understand, Jim. You hate everyone, and now I know that includes me too. I never should've told you how I felt. I'm such an idiot!" she yelled, hugging herself and shivering from the cold as she resumed crying with deep sobs that made it hard for her to breathe.

Jim reached over and pushed the start button, then turned the heat setting to its maximum.

"No, Angela. You're wrong."

She took a few ragged breaths and gained control of her voice for a moment.

"Okay. If you don't hate me, then you tolerate me. Forgive me if that doesn't make me feel any better. I'm the last girl on earth for all practical purposes and you could never be with me." She dropped her head to the steering wheel and resumed crying. He was hopeless.

"That's not what I meant," Jim spoke through his teeth. He grabbed one of his hands with the other and began wringing them. He bit at his top lip and looked around as if someone could help him say what he felt but couldn't find words for.

Without lifting her head from the top of the steering wheel, she asked through her tears, "Then what, Jim? Am I just not attractive enough? That would explain why we've been nothing more than friends for so long." She lifted her head and tried to blot the tears from her eyes with her arm.

"I could never be with you… because I'm not good enough for you, Angela."

She took her arm away from her face and looked at him, narrowing her eyes. "What are you talking about?

Now that Jim had found the words, he knew how to say what he was feeling.

"Angela, I can't be with you because you're too good for me. You're the most precious thing on this earth. You're the best person - the only good person I've ever known. Yeah, I really do hate people, Angela, but not you. You're the one person I could never hate." He looked quickly away, then back at her like he'd just quickly decided something. A tear rolled down from one of his eyes. "I love you, Angela. I would give my life for you, and with the way things are going, I probably will someday soon, just to make sure you go on living so there will be one good thing in this rotten, fucked up world. As long as you're in the world, then whatever crazy cosmic power exists out there will have to preserve it. You're beautiful, Angela. You're an angel to me. That's why I can't be with you. You deserve someone a million times better."

Angela's tears stopped as she listened to Jim. The shock and pain she felt when Jim said he couldn't be with her was replaced by a feeling of numbness. Jim loved her. He had always loved her.

"I don't need or want someone better than you. I just want *you*, Jim." She reached for him and he reached for her. They held each other, leaning over the center console and shivering in the frozen car. He whispered in her ear with his lips so close that her hair moved as he spoke.

"I'm messed up, Angie. You *don't* want me."

She took his head in her hands and moved it so his face was right in front of hers. She looked intently into his eyes.

"I *do* want you, Jim. I love you. You're all I've ever wanted."

Jim moved his head back beside hers. He didn't want her to see him cry. But she could feel him crying as he held her tightly.

Four

Monica looked around for help. There was only the house on the corner. The gravel road they were on ran between empty lots covered with weeds and snow. Nothing behind them but the highway and the mountain. She climbed over the back seat and then crawled through the space between the front bucket seats.

She looked out of the broken window at the house for any sign that someone was home. There was a motorhome in the long, wide driveway but no other cars. And there was a man lying in the grass, unconscious and bleeding.

"Trey!" she shouted.

Adrenaline coursed through her veins and she burst into action, reaching for the door handle on the passenger side of the van. She hopped out and landed on the thin layer of snow and ran to Trey. She kneeled in the snowy grass next to him and looked at his blood-covered face. She could see the fog from his breath. He was alive.

"Oh God, I need help. HELP ME!" she cried out.

There was no one around to hear her. She stood up and carefully ran to the front door of the one-story house. She grabbed the knocker with cold, shaking hands and slammed it down on the brass plate repeatedly, begging someone to answer the door.

"Please," she moaned.

She let go of the knocker and made her hands into fists and pounded on the door. No one came. She looked at the RV and dared to hope as she ran over to it. She grabbed onto a chrome handle and pulled herself up onto the step below the driver's side door and reached for the handle. It opened.

"Thank you, thank you, thank you," she whispered.

She climbed onto the driver's seat and leaned over in search of the ignition and wanted to hug God when she saw it. The key was in the ignition. She turned the key and had never been so happy to hear the sound of an engine come to life.

She looked at the instrument panel to see how full the tank was and she watched the temperature gauge rise rapidly to the halfway point. Someone had been running the engine not long ago. And the tank was full. Monica figured the owner must've been planning a trip and would probably be back soon, but surely they would understand her predicament. It was an emergency. She wasn't trying to steal anything.

She went into the back of the RV and to the side door, exiting and setting the door to stay open. Now she had to try to get Trey inside. She knew it was best not to move an injured person, so dragging one was probably really bad. But she had no choice.

She ran back to Trey and was relieved to see that he was still breathing. Small puffs of vapor briefly appeared in front of his nose. Even smaller wisps of steam rose from the blood flowing from his head. She had to do this quickly so she could stop the bleeding.

She stood behind Trey's head, squatted, then hooked her hands under his armpits and simultaneously lifted and pulled as she started walking backwards. She was able to drag him, but slowly, and it required all of her strength. Trey was thin, but he was dead weight, and he was wet from the snow. Her frozen feet pushed hard into the freezing ground with every step. Her hands, arms and feet hurt from the effort but she didn't stop dragging him until she reached the driveway. When the resistance increased from his waist scraping against the pavement, she gently lowered his head to the ground so she could rest.

She stood there breathing hard and willing her arm muscles to stop hurting. She looked behind her and saw the steady stream of exhaust coming from the RV's tailpipe. Her lip stung where it was split. She licked it and tasted blood. She turned back and looked down at Trey. Still breathing. Still bleeding.

Two hours ago she was sitting in her warm and boring house wondering if she could make it into town for some shopping before the storm arrived. The forecast called for three days of rain and sleet. It was going to be a long, boring weekend. And now look at her. She wondered how she ended up here, doing this.

Once again, she took hold of Trey's inert body from under his armpits and dragged him backwards, careful to keep his dangling head above the ground as she pulled him across the driveway. She rounded the back corner of the RV and continued dragging him toward the side door. Her muscles screamed for relief, but she didn't stop until she reached her goal.

Then she laid his head down again, exhausted and out of breath. "Now for the hard part."

It took longer for her to catch her breath this time and for her heart to slow down. The pain in her arms had reduced slightly, but wasn't going away. She knew she had strained her muscles and the pain was only going to get worse. After a few deep breaths and visualizing what she intended to do, she straddled Trey's body and slid her hands under his back. She pulled him upward so he appeared to be sitting while she hugged him in a kneeling position.

She slid her right foot forward until it was flat on the ground, then she did the same with her left. Now she was hugging him in a very low squat. She squeezed her arms around him as hard as she could. Using all of the strength she could muster, she stood up, pulling Trey up with her. Her arms were wrapped tightly around him, hugging him to her body. She fought to keep her balance as his weight tilted one way then another. She rotated her body until her back was to the door of the RV, then she slowly backed up a few steps until she felt the ridge of the floor against her butt, then she sat and laid down backwards in a barely controlled fall.

She felt like she had no more energy left in her to complete the job, but she pushed that feeling out of her mind, telling herself she could do this. She was almost done. Trey's weight on top of her was making it hard to breathe. She had to finish getting him in. Resting wasn't an option. She breathed as deep as she could and with her palms on the floor, forced herself to scoot backwards and out from under Trey. As she scooted past him, his blood dripped on her face, shirt and pants.

She wiped Trey's blood off her face with her arm, smearing it across her cheek toward her ear. She looked at his body half in and half out of the RV. She was determined to bring him in the rest of the way so she could shut the door and let the heat start building up. She grabbed him beneath his armpits again and dragged him inward and toward the back of the RV. When his feet cleared the doorway, she set him down and closed the door.

She sat on the seat in front of the dining table to rest. She was too exhausted and out of breath to cry so she forced herself to think of what she needed to do next. Ten minutes later she had him on the bed. She got a towel from the bathroom, folded it and put it on his head, then she lay down next to him to rest for a minute and wait for the warm air to reach them.

Five

Carl had difficulty seeing with the slushy rain smacking his face and sticking to the windshield. He couldn't find a way to turn the wipers on so he had to look out the side window or up over the windshield, and every time he did that, he got more wet snow in his eyes. It was really starting to piss him off. He pulled over at the first place he saw.

The row of diagonal parking spaces in front of the Mile High Tavern was empty. Carl pulled into the space closest to the door. It was a handicapped space, which Carl thought would never matter again.

"Fuck a bunch of gimps," he said as he got out of the car, eager to get inside and out of the damned snowy rain.

He pulled the door open and stepped into the dark interior that was weakly lit by two kerosene lanterns. A small, half-bald, skinny man with no chin was standing behind the bar taking money out of the cash register. He looked up at Carl and froze.

Carl looked at him then quickly moved his eyes left and right checking to see if there was anyone else inside. There wasn't.

"We're… we're closed!" the man stammered, blinking at Carl and not moving. He looked like a mannequin with cash in his trembling hands.

"You need to start a damned fire in this place. It's freezing in here." Carl didn't care if they were closed or not. No one was going to give him orders unless they were backed up by the barrel of a gun. He walked up to the bar and sat down on a stool.

"I need a beer and I need it now. Make it a draft. Tall."

The man behind the bar unfroze. He put the money he was holding in his pants pocket and looked around. He saw the draft beer spigots and then looked behind him and saw rows of glasses on the counter.

"You ain't even a bartender, are you?"

"I'm... I'm the owner," the man lied, his voice pitched high with fear.

"Bullshit. Give me a fucking beer before I come back there and rip your head off."

The man swallowed and plucked a glass from the counter with shaking hands.

"I said tall!" Carl bellowed.

The man saw his error and put the short glass down and grabbed a larger one. He walked over to the spigots and eyed the several handles with various names and logos. He looked at Carl, his eyes wide with fear and uncertainty.

"Give me a Hef," Carl said.

The man looked again at the taps and saw one that said Hefeweizen and put the glass under the spigot and pulled the tap down. The glass filled and foam rose rapidly to the top. When the foam threatened to overflow, he released the tap and brought the beer over to Carl. He set it down on the bar in front of him, foam sloshing over onto Carl's hand.

Carl backhanded the man, which spun him around. He grabbed hold of the counter behind him to keep from falling, knocking over a few glasses which fell to the floor and bounced on the grimy rubber mat.

"Are you a fucking retard?" Carl growled at him.

Carl saw a dirty bar towel folded into a neat rectangle sitting next to a Zippo lighter beside the cash register. He picked up the towel, shook it out and wiped the foam off his hand, then used it to dry his face. It smelled like old beer poured into an ashtray.

The man behind the bar was staring at him, waiting to see what he would to do next. Carl threw the towel at his face. The man jerked, startled, and caught the towel.

Carl got up and walked around the bar. The man started walking backwards, certain that Carl was going to attack him. But Carl grabbed a tall glass and went to the taps and poured himself a proper beer. Then he went back around to sit down on his stool.

"Now get me some Marlboros from the vending machine," he said as he sat down.

The man quickly went to the register and grabbed all of the quarters, then rushed over to the vending machine on the far side of the bar below a sign that said Restrooms with an arrow pointing down a short, dark hall.

He saw that the machine took dollar bills so he put the quarters in his pocket and pulled out the cash he had taken and tried to insert a dollar bill but the machine wouldn't pull it in like it was supposed to.

"There ain't no 'lectricity, you dumbfuck."

"But, you're the one who said to use the vending machine," the man countered.

Carl got up and started walking toward him. The man raised his hands in front of his face and blinked rapidly. Carl turned to the right, ignoring him and went down the dark hall. He found a locked door, stepped back a bit, then kicked at it with the heel of his boot, aiming left of the doorknob. He disappeared through the doorway, then reappeared a minute later carrying a carton of cigarettes.

"Sometimes you gotta use your brain," he said as he passed the man who was still cowering next to the vending machine.

Carl sat down, ripped open the carton, removed a pack, unwrapped it and lit a cigarette with the Zippo lighter. He took a long drink of his beer and sighed, finally able to relax and enjoy himself. He would've liked to have some music but he knew that wasn't going to happen.

He looked at his dim reflection in the flickering light from the lanterns in the dingy mirror behind the bar. His face was swollen and bruised with two black eyes and his hair was wet and wild from having driven in the convertible. He looked like some kind of monster. He liked that. He could see why the little man was so scared of him as soon as he walked in.

"Hey you! What's your damn name?"

"Jeffrey," the man immediately replied. "Jeffrey Cordigan."

"I'm Carl. Why don't you look behind the bar for something to snack on and get yourself a beer and be civil?"

Jeffrey went behind the bar and found a bag of peanuts. He set them down on the bar and grabbed a small glass, then traded it for a tall glass and poured himself a beer. He tilted the glass the way he'd seen Carl do it but still ended up with a beer that was half foam. He came around the bar and took a stool a few seats away from Carl and sucked the foam off the top of his beer.

"Nice to meet you, Carl."

Carl looked at him, squinting his eyes and shaking his head.

"I know you came here for the cash. But did you see a gun behind the bar? Maybe a shotgun?"

"No. Just a bat."

Carl poured peanuts out onto the bar and began cracking them open and dropping the shells on the ground, alternately popping peanuts in his mouth and taking large swigs of his beer.

"Whaddaya think yer gonna do with the money?"

The man looked around nervously. He wasn't comfortable with a casual discussion of his thieving. "I… I don't know yet."

"You *did* see the bomb, right?"

Jeffrey nodded vigorously.

"Obviously, that's why you came here. You know there ain't no law to stop you."

More nodding from Jeffrey.

"You don't need money. The 'conomy just took a big dump. Might makes right from now on. What you need is a gun."

"You know, Abraham Lincoln said, 'Let us have faith that right makes might,' and I think-"

"I wasn't kidding about the fire."

"Huh?"

"Start a damn fire in the fireplace! I can see my fuckin' breath."

Six

Thunder cracked and rumbled and a torrent of rain pelted the roof of the motorhome, startling Monica out of her sleep. She had only meant to rest for a minute before tending to Trey's wound. Now she worried that he may have bled to death while she napped right next to him. She went to remove the towel from his head and it was stuck. She put it back down, grimacing and hoping she hadn't reopened the wound.

She wanted to get the towel wet to see if she could pull it away from the wound without pulling away the clotted blood with it. She went into the small bathroom and turned on the faucet. As she had feared, there was no water. She could hear plenty of water falling above her head though. She just needed a way to get some.

She went in to the kitchen of the RV and found a plastic cup in a cabinet. She went outside and looked in both directions and saw water pouring off of a rain spout attached to the gutter on the RV's roof. She ran over to it and caught a cupful and went back in.

She slowly poured the water into the towel and was able to unstick it from Trey's head. She saw that the blood on his head was shiny in places, but it didn't appear to be bleeding. She was glad that it stopped on its own. She was not good at dealing with blood and injuries. She assumed that the wound should probably be cleaned but she wasn't up to the task. Her goals had been to get Trey out of the cold rain, and to stop the bleeding.

She sat on the bed looking at him and remembered hearing some warning about people with head wounds. She wasn't sure what she knew about that. Then she remembered what it was: never let a person with a concussion go to sleep. No, that couldn't be right. People had to sleep eventually. But she was sure that a person was supposed to be kept awake for some period of time after a concussion. She wondered if the same rule applied if the person had been knocked unconscious and remained unconscious for a few hours. To be safe, she decided she better wake him up.

First she took off her soaking wet socks and put them in the bathroom sink. The skin on her toes felt funny. She lifted a foot and saw that her toes were white and wrinkled. She felt dumb for falling asleep with wet socks on. She went back to Trey and wasn't sure how to wake him. He might have other injuries that weren't visible. What if she pushed his chest and he had a broken rib? She assumed that since he had landed head first, his feet were probably uninjured so she grabbed one of Trey's boots and started shaking it.

"Trey. Wake up."

Trey groaned and rolled over onto his side, pulling his feet away from her and bending his knees into a fetal position. Monica looked at him for a second then walked to the side of the bed and slapped him on his ass.

"What the hell?" Trey rolled over and was shocked to see Monica standing there looking at him and shaking her hand in pain.

"I'm glad you could feel me spanking your wallet. Welcome back to the land of the living."

"What happened? Where are we?" Trey sat up on the bed and winced in pain. He brought his hand to his head where the pain was and he felt something unexpected. He looked at his hand and saw spots of blood. He looked at Monica, confused.

"You crashed my van into a telephone pole and went flying out the window into a stone wall. You probably have a concussion and need to stay awake."

"Fuck. Really? Where are we? Sounds like an RV in a rain storm."

"It is. The RV is in the driveway right next to where we wrecked. No one was home who could help us, but the keys were in the ignition, so…" She shrugged. "Here we are."

"How did I get in here? You couldn't have carried me."

"You're right. I dragged you. And it wasn't easy. It was probably the hardest thing I've ever done. *And* I had to get you up into this thing after I dragged you to it. How does your head feel?"

"It hurts like a bitch. I don't suppose you have any aspirin, or something stronger maybe?"

"I'll see if I can find anything."

Monica left for a minute and came back carrying a small white plastic case. She set it on the bed and undid the hasp. Inside were paper packets of aspirin and acetaminophen, some gauze, a small pair of scissors and bandages of various sizes. She handed him the aspirin.

"There's some water in that cup over there, but it came from the roof, so it'll probably taste nasty."

Trey opened the packet and tossed the aspirin back in his mouth and worked his saliva around to swallow them without the water.

"You look awful. I'm sorry about what happened to you. I didn't know…" Trey turned away, unable to face her because of his part in the home invasion that led to her being raped.

"You saved me. You stopped him and you got me away from him. You don't have to be sorry."

He looked back at her. "And then I wrecked your van."

"It's insured. As soon as I can get to a phone I'll call the police and the insurance company." Trey look startled. "Don't worry. I won't tell them you were with him. I don't want to get you in trouble. If we can get a ride to my house, I'll wait long enough for you to get away on your motorcycle before calling the police." Trey continued to look at her like there was something wrong.

"Oh shit," he said, leaving his mouth hanging open.

"I promise I won't say anything about you. As far as I know, I owe you my life. I won't do anything to get you in trouble." She sat on the bed and put her hand on his leg. "I don't blame you for what happened. I'm grateful you were there."

"Monica, there ain't no police to call. The phones are down, remember?"

"They could be working by now. You said there was an explosion. How bad could it be?"

"It was really bad. It was more than just an explosion. I mean, it *was* an explosion, but the thing is, it was nuclear." Trey stared at her, waiting to see how she was going to take such terrible news after everything else she'd been through.

"What blew up, and how bad was it?"

"Uh… Denver blew up, and it was as bad as bad can be. It was a *nuclear* explosion, Monica."

"You're not serious. You said the authorities wanted us to evacuate. They wouldn't do that over a nuclear explosion. What *really* happened?"

Trey looked down at the bed. "We made up the part about helping the Sheriff's deputies and needing to evacuate, but Carl wanted to find a house to raid because with Denver bein' destroyed by the nuke, he knew no one could call the cops. And that's why he did what he did to you."

Monica covered her mouth with one hand and froze, staring at Trey. He saw tears start to flow from her eyes but she didn't make a sound. He scooted over to her and put an arm around her. She leaned into him, wrapping her arms around him, and then he heard her crying into his jacket. He lay back on the bed and she went with him.

Trey stayed awake until she cried herself to sleep. Her warmth and closeness gave him something to focus on which helped take his mind off the pain in his head. He stroked her hair from her head down to her lower back where it came to an end. After a while, he slept too.

Seven

Carl drank while Jeffrey built a fire. After a while, the tavern got warmer and felt less damp. Carl drank quickly out of boredom and because the beer was free. Eventually, he could barely keep himself upright on his stool.

"I'm gonna lay down in the office. Wake me up when the rain stops. I need to find a gun somewhere and take care of some business." He slid off his stool and grabbed the bar to steady himself, then walked toward the dark hall.

"Supposed to rain for three days though," Jeffrey said.

Carl stopped.

"Are you shittin' me?"

"I shit you not," Jeffrey replied, suppressing an urge to giggle. He'd always found that expression to be very funny but he feared Carl would think he was indeed shitting him if he laughed.

Carl turned around.

"Three fuckin' days?"

"From what I heard, yes." When Carl glared him, he lost the urge to laugh.

"Aw fuck! Don't wake me up at all then." Carl continued down the hall and disappeared into the hallway that just barely caught some of the flickering light from the fireplace so it wasn't completely dark.

A few minutes later, Jeffrey heard Carl snoring and he wondered if he should slip away from the tavern. He had only come for the money in the register and he had gotten that. He was surprised that Carl hadn't taken it from him. He was a pretty bossy guy, and abusive too. Jeffrey admitted to himself that Carl scared him.

He should leave while the big man was asleep, but he didn't really have anywhere to go and he didn't like the idea of walking back in the rain to his friend's house where he was over-extending his stay on the couch. He could probably find a house whose owners were in Denver when the bomb went off and wouldn't be coming back. That's what he'd do. He just needed the rain to stop, then he'd find a car.

Maybe he ought to stick with Carl for a little while. They might be able to help each other. Carl was looking for a gun. Jeffrey knew where they could find guns. Easy peasy. Maybe if he helped Carl get a gun, Carl would help him get a car.

Jeffrey walked over to the tavern door to see what Carl was driving. He pulled the door open and it swung inward, driven by the force of a strong wind that was blowing the rain almost horizontally. He got a quick glance at Carl's ride and pushed the door shut, putting his shoulder into it, fighting against the wind that was trying to push it open.

He couldn't believe Carl was driving a convertible with the top removed. It was a fantastic looking car, but they definitely weren't going anywhere in it until this rain stopped.

When Carl came shuffling out of the dark hallway later that evening, he found Jeffrey sitting next to the fire struggling to read a paperback he had found behind the bar. Carl couldn't believe it. The guy was reading a book, and in the dark no less.

"Hey, Jimmy!" Carl yelled.

"It's Jeffrey," he said, looking up from his book and hoping Carl didn't take offense at being corrected.

"Whatever. I don't want to sit around this place for two more days. Where's the nearest gun store or pawn shop?"

Jeffrey put his book down on the hearth. "I don't know about that, but I know a place not far from here where there's plenty of guns and all the food you could possibly want."

"What kinda place?" Carl was behind the bar now, pouring himself a beer.

"It's a small community of Mormons, barely a mile from here."

"Why the fuck would a buncha Mormons have guns and food?"

"They have to. Their church requires it. I guess it must have to do with the End Times or something."

"How do you know about this?"

"Well, I've been kind of down on my luck lately, and a Mormon I know told me where I could get some help from his church. So I went there and they gave me some food and clothes and so I did some work for them. That's when I heard that they store at least a year's worth of food in their basements, and there was plenty of talk about guns too."

"That sounds perfect. When I finish this beer, you're gonna show me where this place is."

"In the rain?"

Mocking him, Carl replied in a whiny voice, "Yes, in the *rain*! I told you, I ain't sittin' around here for two fuckin' days. I need a gun. I got business I gotta tend to."

They drove up the highway covered with garbage bags that Jeffrey turned into makeshift ponchos. The plastic rippled and fluttered in the heavy wind. Carl felt stupid wearing a garbage bag but he conceded that he was much drier than he'd be without it. Jeffrey told him where to turn off the highway and they followed a winding road more than a mile into the woods.

The tree-lined road came to an end at an intersection that looked like a roundabout but with a large grassy circle half walled off with bricks. They could turn left or right to go around it. In various places throughout the wall, there were square holes like portals. On the other side of the walled off circle there was a Mormon temple. Streets lined the sides of the temple which were accessible from the roundabout entrance where Carl was pulling up.

"This is it. Pull over," Jeffrey ordered without thinking. Carl scowled at him, but did as Jeffrey instructed.

"I planned on pulling over," he said, daring Jeffrey to doubt him. "Now what?"

"Well, I guess we gotta get into one of those houses without drawing any attention. Any one of them should do. We can get guns, food and a car and then get away before anyone finds out what we were here."

Carl pushed his wet hair back and mopped water off his forehead. His eyelids lowered as he tried to think of a strategy. He thought they should back the car up till it was out of view, then try sneaking back into the compound through the trees on the right and emerge behind one of the houses. He didn't think to tell Jeffrey his plan. He was just going to do it. He reached for the ignition to start the engine but stopped when he heard a bell toll.

He looked at the temple where the sound was coming from. After three gongs, the bell stopped. Men ran out of from the houses and went out of view behind the brick wall in front of the temple. All of them were carrying either rifles or handguns. Some had both.

"Ah shit! What kinda church people run around with guns?"

"They're pretty nice people," Jeffrey answered.

"Shut up, you idiot."

A bearded face appeared in the center portal that looked directly onto the intersection where Carl had stopped the car.

"Hello!" the man shouted. "Do we know you?"

Carl and Jeffrey looked at each other then looked back at the man. Neither of them spoke. Carl was trying to think fast. This was a lot more difficult than bullshitting his way into someone's house.

"Are you FLDS?" the man inquired after getting no response to his first question. He gave them only a few seconds to respond. "You're gonna want to turn that car around and head back the way you came. This here's private property."

Carl didn't know if they should bother trying to talk their way in and then try to overpower someone, or just find something easier like he and Trey had done yesterday. He thought he might at least try bluffing a little and pretending they were lost and hungry, but before he made up his mind, the man's face moved away from the portal and the barrel of a rifle came through it with the man holding it up to his shoulder and looking through the iron sights.

"Ya'll just go on now," he yelled.

"Fuck it," Carl spat. These people didn't fuck around. He started the engine. He backed the car up and was half way through a 3-point turn when he spotted a car coming down the road from behind them. He left his car sideways, blocking the road and quickly got out and ran toward the approaching vehicle waving his arms above his head as if he needed assistance.

The oncoming car slowed to a stop thirty feet away. It was an old station wagon with two women in it. The man behind the brick wall yelled something but Carl couldn't make out what he was saying, but it sounded like he was trying to warn the women off. Carl ran up to the driver's window.

"There's a snake in my car rattling its tail at my friend and he's scared to move. You don't have a pistol I could borrow, do you? It might save his life!"

The woman in the passenger seat quickly opened the glove compartment and took out a twenty-two caliber pistol and carefully handed it across the car to Carl.

"Hurry," she said. "We'll pray for your friend."

Carl accepted the weapon, thumbed off the safety and said, "Thank you. Now get the fuck out of the car. Both of you. Nice and slow."

The women looked at each other in shock that they had just been betrayed by what they had assumed were members of their congregation. This man was not a Saint.

"Get out of the car, now!"

The driver looked at Carl standing in the rain getting drenched. "We need to get our umbrellas from the backseat. Can you give us a second?"

"No, you need to get the fuck out of the car before I shoot you in the face."

They saw the man behind the portal shaking his head and gesturing to someone behind him. The driver opened her door and Carl grabbed her as she stepped out. He pulled her in front of him, holding her there by her upper arm. "You!" he said to the other woman. "Get in front of her and start walking up to that red car, slowly."

The other woman did as she was told. Carl and his hostage followed directly behind her. Within seconds the women were soaked and chilled from the incessant wind. When they reached the car, he yelled to the man with the rifle, "We just need a few guns. Send someone out with a few and you can have your women back!" He was going to say he wanted something better than a .22 but he didn't want to advertise the caliber of the gun he was holding.

Behind the wall, the men huddled together. The man at the portal stayed where he was and told the others what he was observing. A brief discussion took place about how to handle the situation. Most of the men were willing to make the trade that Carl demanded. One man was opposed to trading and had a better idea.

"He's got my wife out there. If we just give them what they want, what's to keep them from coming back again when they want something else?" he asked the group.

"We weren't prepared for this, Noah. After we get rid of these two, we'll build a barricade at the intersection and we'll post guards."

"That's fine for later, Stephen, but he's got my wife and Sean's wife and he needs to be dealt with right now," Noah replied.

"How do you propose to deal with him? He's using your wife as a shield."

"The one in the car is unarmed and hasn't even moved. I can take out the big one who has my wife's .22. It's an easy shot from this distance."

Carl yelled across the distance, "I'm giving you thirty seconds and then one of these ladies is gonna get shot. Ya hear me?"

"Are you sure you can hit him in this wind?"

"Yeah. Someone back me up at the next portal, just in case I miss. But I won't."

Noah turned around and relieved the man at the central portal. That man ran to the left and stopped at the next portal and propped his rifle up there, taking aim at Carl. He didn't want to shoot though with Noah's wife standing in front of the man with the gun, and Sean's wife standing in front of her. It would be too easy to miss and hit one of the women.

Noah took aim and yelled through the portal.

"Let them go and we'll give you whatever you want!" Noah hoped that the man would be at least a little distracted by their refusal to give in, and by having a counter-offer to consider. He sighted in the man's head and squeezed his trigger.

Carl's face was sprayed with blood and bits of brain and bone fragments at the same instant he heard the shot fired from behind the wall.

"Oh dear God!" Noah screamed and collapsed, falling to the ground in a wave of shock, grief and guilt. "What have I done?"

Carl fired back at the portal as the woman he was holding collapsed in front of him. The other woman screamed, "Oh my goll!" and ran to the left past Carl's car and kept running alongside the border hedges on the south side of the property, never looking back. Another man took up Noah's place at the portal and began firing a pistol at Carl.

Jeffrey ducked down in the car. Carl's shots sent pieces of brick flying off the wall as he missed the portal with every shot. He ran backwards toward the station wagon as he fired. Halfway there, his pistol clicked. He was out of ammo.

The men behind the wall were firing repeatedly at him. He heard a bullet whiz past his head. Carl figured they were pretty shitty with their weapons as he turned around to run the rest of the way to the station wagon. Then one of them proved him wrong with a shot that hit him in the back and caused him to turn more than he had intended. He fell down facing his car where Jeffrey was still ducked down out of sight.

Carl crawled the remaining few feet to the station wagon and pulled himself inside, trying to keep his head low. The engine was still running. He honked the horn twice. Jeffrey popped his head up to look toward the station wagon. Carl gestured for him to come. The passenger door of the Roadster opened and Jeffrey ran toward Carl. He had only gone a few steps before Carl watched a cloud of red mist fly out of Jeffrey's face and then he appeared to dive, his body pitching forward and sliding a few feet on the asphalt.

"Looks like he's fucked," Carl said and moved the gearshift into Reverse. He put his right arm on the top of the bench seat and turned his head to look behind him as he drove backwards. He knew he'd been shot, but he didn't feel anything yet. Maybe he wasn't hit that bad, he thought.

Eight

Monica woke without opening her eyes. She felt safe for the first time in years. She lay there with her arm around Trey feeling his warmth and the slight movement from his breathing and she listened to the rain pattering on the roof.

Trey had said that Denver was nuked. She didn't know what he meant exactly and she didn't want to know. It was too much to think about. Nothing in life was the way it was supposed to be. It was easier to just lie here with her eyes closed and let this small space be her whole world.

There was a time when she had loved life and had dreams of the future. When she was in college, she didn't know what she wanted to do. Then she met Thomas and everything fell into place. She quit school and got married. They moved to the mountain house he had inherited from an aunt. She got pregnant and suddenly knew what her life was supposed to be about. She was going to be a mother. The thought of having a child filled her with happiness.

But then she had the miscarriage and her dream was ripped away from her. All she had left was Thomas. But then the war took him away, leaving her all alone. After that she just went through the motions of life, not really caring what happened and not daring to dream. Eventually she settled in to the routine patterns of living. Occasionally she even painted, but without passion or inspiration.

Alone on the mountain, it was peaceful and safe. Life was not good, but as long as she had nothing and wanted nothing, she never had to fear losing anything. She did not look forward to the future and she tried not to think about the past. She simply lived day to day; secure in her knowledge that life could not get worse than it already had.

Then Carl and Trey appeared on her doorstep. Life took another unexpected turn for the worse. And now, unbelievably, she was doing something she thought she'd never do again. She was lying on a bed with a man, and feeling safe and comfortable. The greatest irony to her was that he was one of the men who had invaded her home. She believed him though when he said that he didn't know that Carl was going to do what he did.

The fact that he had saved her from his friend gave him credibility. And now she had saved him too. She could tell him that they were even now and they could go their separate ways, but she felt that they still needed each other to continue surviving - at least for a while. She looked at Trey sleeping and felt anxious again about him being asleep so soon after a serious head injury. She gently patted his chest where her hand was resting.

"Trey. Wake up."

Trey moaned something unintelligible.

"I'm sorry, but I think it's better if you don't sleep yet." She patted him again a little harder.

"What? What's going on?" He looked at her, blinking rapidly, trying to focus.

"I think we should go somewhere. We can't just stay in this RV forever. It's going to run out of gas eventually."

"You're right." He struggled into a sitting position and squeezed his eyes shut as the pain in his head returned. "I'd rather stay asleep because then I don't feel the pain, but I've got to find my sister, and you need to find your husband."

"I know where my husband is. He's not going anywhere." Monica looked down and pursed her lips.

"That's great. I need to head south to my parent's cabin. Which direction is your husband?"

"He's in Fort Logan," she answered quietly.

"What? Fort Logan, the cemetery?"

"Yes. He was killed in Afghanistan two years ago."

"Oh God. I'm sorry." Trey leaned forward and put his arms around her. She held him and rested her head on his shoulder. She thought she would cry and was surprised when she didn't. She just felt the same numb grief she'd felt since Thomas's funeral. It was an internally cold feeling. Cold and lonely. Holding Trey made her feel better for the first time since Thomas died.

"Is there somewhere you want me to take you?" Trey asked.

Monica pulled away to look at Trey. "I don't have anywhere to go but home, but now I don't know if it's safe there. And… I'm afraid to be alone."

"You don't have to be. You can come with me to my parent's cabin. It's not far from here. We should go now before the rain freezes. I would really hate to drive this thing down the mountain with ice on the road."

"Can we look at my house and see if he's still there? I need some shoes." She looked down at her bare feet.

"Oh shoot! I didn't get any shoes when I grabbed some stuff for you."

"It's okay. I appreciate what you did for me. No one would expect you to be thinking about proper attire."

"Let's go take a look and see if his bike is still there. Maybe he left since it's been raining. Riding a bike in the rain really sucks, but at least it's possible. Driving in the snow is pure suicide. Carl says he can do it, but that's total bullshit."

Trey stood up and reached out for the wall as a wave of dizziness washed over him and he felt a pulsing pain in his head.

"Oh shit. I don't think I can drive. Can you handle this thing?"

"I don't know. Maybe if I go real slow."

"Well, I don't want you racin' down the mountain anyway."

She laughed and got up to help steady him, putting her arm around his waist. They walked together to the front of the RV. He sat in the passenger seat and she took the driver seat. She sat there staring at the console, trying to confront the idea of driving this behemoth of a vehicle.

"It's just a car," Trey said. "Only bigger. Don't let it intimidate you."

"Okay. Here we go..."

"Just take it real slow. We're in no rush and we don't have far to go."

Monica backed out of the driveway very carefully, then drove forward and turned left onto the highway, very slowly accelerating until she reached 25 m.p.h., then she held it there.

"I don't want to go any faster than this."

"That's fine. There's no traffic up here, so don't worry. Nice and easy."

Trey still felt dizzy and foggy-headed so he was fine with the slow speed as long as he didn't have to do the driving. He'd already crashed once. He was not going to risk it again. He wasn't sure how they were going to deal with checking her house to see if Carl was there. They should've thought more about that and come up with a plan before heading out.

If nothing else, he figured they could turn onto Monica's street and use the RV's high beams to see if Carl's bike was there. But even if it was, that didn't mean for sure that Carl was there. He could be in a neighbor's house, or could have taken someone's car and driven away while it was still snowing. He would've only risked leaving on his bike if it was raining, and he'd be reluctant to do that. He could manage it with his goggles and gloves, but he'd get soaked without a change of clothes.

Headlights appeared behind them as they were approaching the intersection of Monica's street. This ordinary occurrence was much more significant now since there were so few people on the mountain. As Monica slowed down, the car behind them increased its speed. She and Trey watched in their side-view mirrors as the car behind them appeared determined to ram right into them.

Monica started to make the left turn onto her street and just then the car zipped around to their left on a collision course with them. She stomped on the brake pedal and Trey flew forward into the windshield, yelling out in pain as his head bounced off of it and he fell back into his seat. The car flew by, just missing the left front end of the RV.

"Shit!"

"Are you alright, Trey? Oh no, you're bleeding again!"

"That was Carl!"

"What!? Are you sure?"

Trey wiped dripping blood out of one of his eyes and looked around for something to stop the blood flow.

"I'm pretty sure. I didn't see his face, but I saw his colors."

"What do you mean, his colors?"

Trey pointed a thumb over his shoulder at his back. "His vest. He had an Unforgiven patch on his vest - our colors."

"But could it have been someone else from your... group?"

"It could've been, but I think it was Carl. All of the guys except him and me live in Denver, and we know Carl was up here."

"Do you think he saw us?"

"Not a chance. He flew by like a maniac. He wasn't looking backwards."

"Well if he's zooming down the mountain, then it's safe to go my house." She took her foot off the brake and let the car move forward at idle speed. Her hands were shaking from the encounter with the speeding station wagon and Trey getting hurt again.

Trey found a microfiber cloth in the compartment in front of his seat and held it to his head. It quickly turned red as it absorbed his blood. Carl's bike was in the street in front of Monica's driveway.

"Oh no. Both motorcycles are there. What if that wasn't him in the car?" She stopped the RV in front of the neighbor's house next to hers. "What should we do?" She held her hand on the gearshift lever, ready to put it in Reverse.

"I'm going to get out and walk around your house and see if it looks like anyone is inside."

"But what if he's there and he sees you?"

Trey pulled the gun out of the back of his waistband. "If he's still here, I'm armed, and he's not."

"I forgot you had my gun." She smiled.

"I'll give it back in a few minutes."

"No. Keep it. I only fired it once when Thomas was teaching me how to shoot."

"I'll be back in a few minutes. Keep the doors locked just in case. If anyone approaches who isn't me, honk the horn like crazy and I'll come running."

"Be careful. You're still bleeding and you probably have a new concussion." Monica looked at him wide-eyed with fear and concern. She didn't want him to put himself in danger, but neither did she want to endanger herself. She hoped to never see Carl again as long as she lived - not unless she was looking at his corpse.

After three minutes that felt like thirty, she saw a figure slowly approaching the RV. The headlights were still on, but he was too far to the left of the beams to be visible. She placed her hand on the horn and stared intently at the dark figure, waiting for him to reach the light.

As he crossed the front of the RV and was illuminated by the headlights, she relaxed, seeing that it was Trey. He came around the side, opened the door and climbed up onto the seat.

"No one's there. The front door was still wide open and no lights are on." He stopped talking to catch his breath and to wipe the sweat and blood from his face with his shirtsleeve.

He gestured for her to go ahead and pull up to the house. She put the RV in Drive and let it slowly roll forward, knocking Carl's bike over and pushing it forward. She stopped when the doors were parallel to her front door. They went inside cautiously and slowly as if neither of them was certain that the house was empty. Trey held the Glock in front of him, prepared to shoot if anyone rushed at them from the dark interior.

"Have you got candles?"

"Yes. We just have to feel our way to the kitchen. Get behind me and hold on to my shirt. You can't afford to hit your head again."

Trey reached into his pocket and pulled out his lighter. He felt for Monica's arm, found it and followed it down to her hand where he deposited the lighter.

"Lead the way," he said, smiling in the dark.

After they found and lit several candles, placing them in key spots throughout the house, Trey laid himself down on the couch at Monica's insistence while she started a fire in the fireplace. Next she tended to Trey's wound the best that she could with hydrogen peroxide, cheap bandages and scotch tape. Trey fell asleep while Monica heated a can of stew for them on the gas range.

Nine

Carl took off, racing down the road and back onto the highway, pulling into a scenic view area and parking out of view to see if he was being pursued by the Mormons. While he waited, he looked in the back of the wagon and found a box of supplies which included a package of diapers. He opened the package and put a diaper under his shirt where he was shot, then pressed his back against the car seat to try to stop the bleeding.

After close to an hour and three saturated diapers, he started feeling lightheaded from the loss of blood. No vehicles passed by on the highway and he concluded that no one was pursuing him. Not yet anyway.

Dusk turned to dark as he waited. He needed to go somewhere to sleep for the night and tend to his bullet wound. He didn't know how he was going to do that, and couldn't think of anyone who could possibly help him.

He knew where to go for a place to sleep though - back to the tavern. There wasn't much there for him and there was nothing special about it, but it's where he'd last been, and like anyone, he was a creature drawn to the familiar. And there was plenty of booze and cigarettes - and food, if he didn't mind eating chips and nuts, which he didn't.

Back at the tavern, Carl added wood to the embers in the fireplace. It took him a while as he only used his right arm to carry wood. Using his left arm caused too much pain as it moved the bullet lodged in his left shoulder blade. His clothes were drenched so he carefully and slowly removed them then laid them in front of the fire. He took another diaper out of the pack and held it behind him as he leaned back against the warm stone wall next to the fireplace.

As soon as he was as comfortable as he was going to get, he wished he had thought to get a tall glass of beer before sitting down. He decided it could wait. He was weak and exhausted from the adrenaline rush during the shootout and the blood loss afterwards. As he drifted off to sleep, he wondered if his mother would help him with the gunshot wound, or would she still be angry at him for knocking her on her ass the last time he'd seen her.

***

After a moment of holding each other in silence, Angela finally pulled away from Jim.

"Let's go inside where we can be more comfortable. I've never seen your room." Her flirtatious smile was barely visible in the moonlight spilling into the car.

"Okay. There's nothing to see but office stuff, but yeah, let's go in." They got out of the car and Jim came around to her side. She linked their hands and they walked slowly to the lodge, each of them feeling that everything was different now. Their lives had been changed first by a nuclear explosion, and now they had just changed again with a kiss.

Jim opened the door and they entered the lodge holding hands. Terry was still working on the pile of goods and looked up. His eyes widened in surprise when he saw Jim and Angela holding hands and looking love-struck.

As the couple walked past Terry, Jim said, "Seems kinda pointless to board up the windows but leave the front door unlocked."

Terry didn't have a comeback for Jim's teasing. He just slowly swiveled his head, watching them as they crossed the main room and went down the hall toward the offices where the three of them had made bedrooms out of offices.

As he got up to lock the door, Terry muttered, "I should've seen that coming."

When they reached Jim's room, he bent down and picked up the candle next to the floorboard. He struck a match and lit the candle then opened the door. He guided Angela over to where his blankets were laid out and set the candle on the floor a few feet away. They sat down facing each other. Jim looked down and away.

"Angie," he said. "Are you sure you-"

"Shut up," she cut him off, pushing him down and climbing on top of him, straddling him. "I don't want to hear anything negative out of you." She leaned down and kissed him. Her hair shrouded his face. He closed his eyes, wondering how long something this good could possibly last before he ended up hurting her somehow.

She raised herself up and removed her jacket, then her shirts, leaving on her bra for the moment. Jim gazed at her in the candlelight and she reached back to her feet, undid her laces and pulled off her shoes. After her shoes were off, she looked down at his smiling face with a smile frozen on her own. Jim couldn't wait anymore and reached for her, pulling her closer and wrapping his arms around her where he could reach the hook to undo her bra. He pulled it away and looked at her.

"You are so beautiful," he whispered.

Angela blushed in the dark, hoping it didn't show in the flickering candlelight. Jim put his left hand on her waist and reached for her with his right hand, gently fondling her left breast, running the back of his fingers against her smooth skin and drawing a circle around the edge of her areola. He lightly gripped her nipple between his knuckles and she sucked in a breath.

He lifted her up so he could get out from under her and quickly took off his jacket and shoes. She lay on her back wondering if this was really happening. Was she about to make love to Jim? She had dreamed of this day but never thought it would come. She knew it never would. But now… it was happening.

Jim straddled her with his knees beside her hips and leaned down to kiss her; one hand quickly returning to her breasts as their tongues explored each other's mouths. Angela had never been happier or more physically aroused. She needed to feel more of him; to explore his entire body with her hands. She wrapped her arms around him, then slipped her hands up under his shirt then slid them up his back and felt long, thick ridges everywhere her hands touched.

"Jim, what are these –" she started to ask.

Jim pulled away from her and rolled over to lie on his back.

"It's nothing!" he snapped. He sounded angry and distant. "I shouldn't have let this happen." Angela turned onto her side, looking at him with concern.

"Jim, what's wrong? *Nothing* happened. We were just kissing and touching. There's nothing wrong with that. Nothing at all."

"I left my shirt on for a reason, Angela. I didn't want you to see… or feel… what they did to me."

Angela scooted closer to him and laid an arm across his chest with her hand on the side of his ribcage, holding him possessively. "Who, Jim? Your parents? Your foster parents? Whatever they did to you wasn't your fault."

"They ruined me, Angie; physically and mentally; inside and out. I told you I'm no good for you."

"That's ridiculous. You *are not* ruined! You may be in need of a good attitude adjustment, but no one ruined you. Don't talk that way."

Jim abruptly sat up, turning his back to her and lifting his shirt.

"Look! And that's just my back. It continues down to my legs. I'm scarred from my shoulders to my thighs. Who could love someone who looks like this?" He pulled his shirt back down, covering the scars.

Angela came up close and wrapped her arms around him from behind.

"I can, Jim. I can love you. I don't care what they did to you. Whatever happened wasn't because you're bad. They didn't make you unlovable." She kissed the nape of his neck then lifted his shirt up and over his head. She thought he'd resist, but he sat there, frozen, taking shallow breaths.

Angela kissed his shoulders, then moved her hands to the back of his neck and massaged there as she kissed his shoulder blades. Her lips met with alternating smooth skin and scar tissue.

"I love you, Jim," she said with her lips against his tortured back.

He suddenly turned around and kissed her fiercely, pulling her close to him, mashing her bare chest against his. Angela was happy that he had found his way through some emotional barrier and was embracing her now, physically and mentally. They heard a pounding on the front door of the lodge. They held still, listening, waiting. The pounding sounded a second time, like somebody very big was banging on the door.

Jim found his shirt and pulled it on while Angela searched for her bra.

"Wait here," he said, and quickly left the room, running down the hall to the large room.

"Someone's at the door," Terry said.

"No shit. Give me a gun."

Terry reached into a box on his left and pulled out a pistol. "You okay with a .45 APC?"

"It's not my first choice, but yeah. I'll take it."

BOOM

BOOM

BOOM

They walked over to the door. Terry stopped to the right of the door and put out his arm to stop Jim from going any further. Terry whispered, "Never stand in front of a door when you don't know who or what's on the other side." He gestured with his gun to indicate the reason why. They could get shot through a door.

"Who's there!?" Terry yelled, louder than necessary, lowering the tone of his voice.

"It's me, Bo! And my momma, Geraldine," a voice replied from outside.

Terry and Jim looked at each other quizzically. Jim thought of saying, "Oh, it's *you*, Bo. Why didn't you say so? Come on in," but he just looked at Terry and waited to see what he would do.

Terry shrugged his shoulders and said, "What do you want?"

"We'd like to come in and dry off if we could. We're soaked out here. Momma looks like somethin' the cat drug in." They heard a wet smacking sound on the other side of the door.

Terry whispered, "I'm going to open the door and see if it's really just a guy and his mother. Step back a few paces and be ready to shoot."

Jim backed up a few steps and tried to turn off his gun's safety. "Just a second." He wasn't having any luck pressing down with his thumb on what he was sure had to be the safety.

"Hold on a second," Terry yelled at the door. He stepped over to Jim and put out his hand for the gun. Jim handed to him and Terry pressed down forcefully in the same place that Jim had been pressing and there was an audible click. He handed it back to Jim and went back to the door. He put his hand on the dead-bolt and looked at Jim, raising his eyebrows to ask if he was ready. Jim nodded.

Terry pulled the door open quickly with one hand and held his pistol pointing upward beside his head with the other. Standing on the porch was the tallest man either of them had ever seen. He was taller than the doorway. The man stepped back and ducked to look in at Terry and Jim. Standing next to him was a woman who was dwarfed by the tall man but was only shorter than average at about five feet, three inches.

The woman looked at Terry with disapproval dripping off of her face along with rainwater. "Well, praise the Lord! Will you let a couple of His children take shelter from the storm?" The scowl never left her face, even as she praised the Lord.

Terry leaned his head over and looked to their right to make sure there was no one else out there. He lowered his gun and said, "Come in." He didn't like that all of their recently acquired supplies were laid out on the floor and in boxes, but he didn't want to make them wait outside while he and Jim stashed everything. "Have a seat by the fire. Jim, help me move this stuff out of the way."

Jim put his gun in his waistband and Terry did the same. They both walked over and began moving boxes over to the table. The man ducked down to enter the lodge and he and his mother left a trail of water as they instinctively walked over to the hearth and sat down. Both of them were shivering. Angela watched them from the hallway with her arms folded across her chest and her feet clad in socks.

After the floor was cleared of supplies, Terry pulled a chair out from the table, sliding it a few feet toward the hearth, then turned it around and sat about ten feet from the couple.

"So what brings you here – on foot and during a storm?"

The tall man answered, "We were heading back to our cabin..."

"My cabin," his mother injected, looking at him as if he should clearly know that the cabin was hers, and hers alone. Jim was still standing by the table. He looked at the woman, considered the expression on her face and the way she talked to her son and decided right then that he didn't like her at all.

"...When our car broke down."

"You mean *my* car?" the woman asked, looking up at her son's face.

"Yes, mother. Your car broke down." He turned his head to look back at Terry. "So we started walking. That was several days ago. We've had to stop frequently because Momma has trouble with her knees."

The woman looked at him with disapproval for revealing a physical condition of hers to total strangers, but stopped short of smacking him.

"Then we saw a sign saying that there was a ski lodge, so we followed the road to the left like the sign said and here we are; cold, wet and thankful for your hospitality."

Terry got up and walked over to them, extending his hand to shake.

"My name is Terry Stepp. It's nice to meet you." He shook hands with Bo and then extended his hand to Geraldine who hesitated at first but then extended one hand, palm down, fingers slightly curled, with her eyes closed. Terry didn't know if she expected him to kiss it as if she was royalty, but he just grasped it lightly and released it.

"We have the Lord to thank for showing us this place," Geraldine said, looking at the ceiling.

"I thought it was just a sign on the road," Jim responded. "Probably put there by mere mortals working for the Department of Transportation."

Geraldine flashed a look of contempt at Jim. Their dislike for each other was now mutual. "We might not have seen the sign if the Lord hadn't showed it to us."

Jim shook his head, certain that he was not going to be able to put up with this for very long. Angela reappeared carrying a mop bucket.

"You guys should wring the water out of your coats," she said, setting the bucket down in front of them. She quickly made her way to Jim's side and put an arm around his waist and distracted him with a kiss before he could make another statement to offend the woman.

"That's Jim and Angela," Terry said, taking advantage of the moment to change the subject. He could see that Jim and Geraldine were going to be a problem. At least Geraldine was. Bo seemed okay.

Geraldine looked at Jim and Angela. Her gaze traveled down to their left hands and their bare ring fingers. Her scowl of disapproval intensified with a slight shaking of her head.

"Pleased to meet you," Bo said, looking at Angela. "Ma'am," he added.

"Is this your lodge, Mr. Stepp?" Geraldine asked.

Terry hesitated for a moment, thinking fast. "Yes it is. You're welcome to stay for the night to dry off, and I can offer you a bowl of soup, and then a ride to your cabin in the morning." He figured that ought to terminate any thoughts they might have about a prolonged stay.

"That would be very good of you, sir," Bo replied.

"With a place this large, surely you have room for two more people," Geraldine said, looking around at the spacious main room and then looking toward the hall that led to multiple offices.

Terry felt very uncomfortable and didn't know how to respond to the woman inviting herself and her son to become long-term occupants of the lodge.

Jim filled the awkward silence. "Terry giving you a ride to your cabin in the morning will beat the hell out of walking. Your knees will appreciate it, and you'll be able to change into dry clothes so you won't look like somethin' the cat drug in."

Geraldine flinched when Jim said "hell." Bo nodded in agreement.

"That would be mighty kind of you," Bo replied, earning another disapproving glance from his mother. They were clearly not on the same page. Geraldine grabbed Bo's sleeve and pulled his head down as she craned hers upward to whisper into his ear.

Once again, Terry felt awkward in their presence as he watched them whispering not more than ten feet away from him. He stood up.

"I'll go fix up some soup. You folks can feel free to lay your coats out in front of the fire after you squeeze the water out of them." He headed toward the kitchen, leaving Jim and Angela to deal with the new guests.

Jim wanted to slip back into his bedroom to get away from Geraldine, but he didn't trust leaving them alone with all of their stuff sitting on the table. That gave him an idea. He picked up a box with spices and seasonings and asked Angela if she would take it to the storage room. He looked intently at her, indicating that she should do it; he had a reason. She took the box and walked down the hall. He slid the heaviest box over closer to himself and waited until he saw her heading back. He picked it up and headed down the hall toward her.

The met at the near end of the hallway and he whispered, "I want to clear our stuff out of there, but with only one of us gone from the room at a time. Grab another box, please," and then resumed walking down the hall before she could answer, carrying the box into the room where they were storing acquired goods.

They continued clearing the table, timing it so that Geraldine and Bo were never alone more than a few seconds. Terry emerged with a large pot of soup and then went back for a tray of bowls and spoons as Angela took the last of the supplies from the table.

When Terry put the bowls on the table, Jim grabbed one and ladled some soup into it.

"No crackers?" he asked Terry.

"Be right back." Terry looked over at the mother and son still seated on the hearth. "Soup's on!"

They walked over and took adjacent seats at the table. Terry returned carrying a red and white box of crackers. Jim reached for the box and took out a package and ripped it open. Terry filled a bowl with soup and slid it in front of Geraldine, then did it again for Bo.

Geraldine brought her hands together in front of her face and looked at Bo. He did the same, closing his eyes. Geraldine closed her eyes and began speaking.

"Our Father, who art in Heaven…"

Jim put a cracker in his mouth then loudly slurped soup from his spoon as she spoke.

"Hallowed be Thy name."

Slurrrrrrp!

"Have you no gratitude for the food He's provided you?"

"Thank you, Terry. I love chicken noodle soup!" Jim said, smiling.

Geraldine was perturbed and abruptly said, "Amen," then touched a finger to the left and right sides of her chest, then her forehead, ending with a touch to her solar plexus. Bo copied her and said, "Amen."

Geraldine looked at Jim as though she was in pain and said, "Would you please pass the crackers?" She looked at the package that he was taking a cracker from with each spoonful of soup.

Jim reached across the table and slid the box of crackers several inches over so that they were now right next to her bowl. He looked at her as if he didn't understand why she needed him to do that.

Angela set her bowl down on Jim's right and took a seat. Jim moved his crackers from his left side to his right to share them with Angela.

"So, where do you folks live?" Terry asked, trying to fill the uncomfortable silence.

"We *did* live in Denver. But now, we'll be staying up in –"

Geraldine interrupted her son. "By the grace of God we were out of town when the bomb went off, destroying our home and our church. After that, the Lord led us up the mountain, and has brought us to this place. We don't know what He has in store for us next."

Jim started laughing. Bo smiled automatically at the sound of laughter and wanted to share in the good humor. "What?" he asked, looking at Jim.

"Nothing. I was just imagining Jesus driving you guys up the mountain road, but I guess you actually drove yourselves - until your car broke down."

Bo was confused. Geraldine sipped her soup. From the look on her face, one would think her bowl was filled with lemon juice.

She looked at Jim. "What faith do you belong to?"

Jim was raising his spoon to his mouth and stopped. He looked directly into Geraldine's eyes. "I'm a nihilist," he said, continuing to stare for a few seconds.

"Well, I suppose you must be happy with what Satan has done to Denver if you believe in annihilation."

Jim shook his head in dismay and said, "I can't do this." He picked up his bowl and walked to the kitchen to finish eating alone.

A few minutes later he came out carrying a mop which he used to clean up the water Bo and Geraldine had tracked in from the front door to the fireplace.

"Cleanliness is next to Godliness," he said, smirking at Geraldine, then set the mop down in the bucket.

He walked down the hall and stopped at his doorway and turned to face the main room. "Terry, wake me up in the morning when you leave to take them to their cabin." He went into his room and shut the door, loudly.

Ten

The next morning when Carl woke up, his neck was stiff with pain. The diaper, stained with dried blood, was sitting beside him. He turned and looked at the stone wall behind him and saw only a few smudges of dried blood on the stones. The bleeding must've stopped. He got up and moved very carefully as he got dressed, aware that too much motion with his left arm could break the clotting loose and the bleeding would resume.

The rain had finally stopped and he needed to find help for his wound in addition to finding Trey for revenge. Trey had it coming even more so now than before. If it wasn't for him taking off with the woman and the gun, Carl wouldn't have had to go looking for a new gun, and he wouldn't have gotten shot. Trey was going to pay for that too.

He knew the road where Trey's parents had a cabin. He didn't know the address, but he knew close enough to where it was and he was sure he'd recognize it when he saw it. There weren't many other places Trey could go. He had to be there.

***

Trey woke up on Monica's couch feeling much better than when he had fallen asleep. He sat up slowly, wary of the pain that he expected to start pounding in his head and was relieved that it had reduced to a dull throb. He looked around Monica's living-room. She wasn't there. He went to the bathroom, glancing in her room as he passed it, but she wasn't in there either. He was a little concerned and as he urinated, he wondered where she could be.

He rinsed his hands, wiped them on a nice towel hanging in a silver hoop on the wall and went back into the hallway. He walked over to the spare bedroom and saw her asleep in the guest bed. It made sense. She didn't want to sleep in her own bed after what had happened there.

He lay down on the bed beside her and adjusted his position until they were perfectly spooned. He put an arm around her with his palm flat on her abdomen. He breathed in the scent of her hair and kissed the back of her head.

"Mmm," she moaned, stirring and rolling onto her back. She opened her eyes and smiled at him. "You look like you're feeling better."

"I am. Thank you. I also feel good enough to drive to my parent's cabin and see if anyone is there."

"Okay," she said.

"I'd like to take some guns from your safe, if you don't mind."

She smiled and spoke a series of numbers. It took him a second to realize what she was saying. He got up slowly and went to the safe. "Tell me again?"

***

After solving the problem of nearly freezing to death, Tori struggled with a new problem; trying to keep Liz entertained without television. She was fortunate that Liz liked to hear the same stories repeatedly, but even Liz had her limits and was getting bored.

She had other problems as well. The woodpile was getting low, and the food was nearly gone. They had to leave soon. She tried to think of where they could possibly go to stay warm and fed, and, she hoped, entertained to some degree. Being with other people would definitely help, especially if they had young kids that Liz could play with.

The only thing she could think of nearby was the Bunny Lodge. It hadn't been scheduled to open until after the bomb went off, but it was possible that some employees could be stranded there. Maybe they wouldn't mind helping a stranger and sharing what had to be a large food supply. And if the place was empty, maybe she could find a way in. She knew there would be plenty of wood there too. At least a couple cords.

She looked outside and saw that the rain had stopped. She took it as an omen telling her it was time to go.

"Liz, honey. Let's get dressed and go for a drive." After they dressed, Tori went to the kitchen and found a pen. She couldn't find any paper but she found a grocery sack. She wrote on the sack and put it on the table, setting the sugar bowl on top of it.

"Let's go see if we can find people," Tori said, escorting Liz to their car.

***

Carl wet his hair in the sink using both hands before he realized what he was doing. He felt the pain in his shoulder-blade as he raised his hands to his head and stopped suddenly when the sharp pain came to life in his shoulder. He turned and looked at his back in the mirror, twisting his head around as far as he could. Dammit. He was bleeding again. But at least it was only oozing out and not gushing like yesterday.

He went and got a diaper and took it into the office, then sat in the leather office chair with the diaper on his bullet hole. He rolled the chair up close to the desk so he could reach the drawers while keeping his back pressed against the chair. He found standard office supplies in most of the drawers. To reach the last drawer, he reclined the chair back a little, then swiveled it, bringing his hand low enough to pull the bottom drawer open.

"There you are!" He slid his hand past a box of ammo and felt around for the gun he hoped to find further back in the drawer, but there was nothing there. He lifted the box of ammo and set it on the desk. It was a box of Smith & Wesson .22LR. "Well at least it's the right caliber," he said. "Thank you, Lord."

After a short while, the bleeding stopped again and he decided to grab a few things and get going. He wanted to take a case of whiskey, but he couldn't carry a case, so he took half a case, carrying two bottles at a time in his right hand. He was able to carry a case of cigarettes one-handed, so he took one, then went back and grabbed the remaining one. He put the cigarettes in the back of the station wagon. The supplies were as good as cash if life didn't return to normal. And he didn't see how it possibly could. Denver was history. There would never be a city there again - at least not for a long, long time.

For the first time, Carl thought about other places. He hoped Denver wasn't the only city that was hit. If it was, then any survivors would just end up migrating to a nearby city. He'd have to either join them, returning to his normal life as a nobody, or stay here and be nothing but a drifter in a ghost town. He may have been overly optimistic when he'd first seen the mushroom cloud the week before.

After loading up the car, he sat behind the wheel thinking while he reloaded his pistol. If he stayed in the mountain area west of Denver, he could still rule the land. Fuck it. That's what he'd do until he found out more about what had happened and how badly America was hurting. He put a diaper under his shirt, placing it over his bullet wound and started the car, heading south in search of Trey's family cabin.

***

Trey took a shotgun and the other Glock from the gun safe. He pulled back the slide on the Glock and saw that the chamber was clear. He released the magazine and saw that it was full as he had expected based on the weight of the gun. He took all of the ammo he could carry and put it in the RV. He came back for the shotgun and found Monica sitting up on the bed.

"We should take the revolver too, just in case one of the Glocks jams. That's why Victor bought it - as a backup."

"Okay. Would you like me to get anything out of your room for you, like some shoes or something?"

"Thank you, but I'll do it."

"Are you sure?"

"Yes. If I can't go in my own room, then he's still victimizing me in a way. You know?

"Yeah."

She got up and gave Trey a hug on her way to her room across the hall. Trey stood watching her, feeling bad for her and imagining what must be going through her mind. He hoped she didn't relive the attack she was still physically recovering from. He wished she would have let him get her things for her.

When she didn't immediately come back out crying, he picked up the shotgun and carried it out to the RV. After that, he didn't know what to do. Should he leave her alone and wait? If he did that, would she think he didn't care? Or should he go in and comfort her? If he did that, would she be insulted, thinking that he didn't believe she was strong enough to confront her demons by herself?

He decided on a compromise. He walked down the hall, stopped outside the door and knocked twice. "I'll be in the kitchen. Okay?"

"Okay," she said.

He couldn't tell if there was anything different in her voice to indicate if she was having difficulty being in her room or not. He sighed and went to the kitchen to find something to eat. He noticed the table was out of place and the salt and pepper shakers were lying on their sides. That was odd. An open pack of bacon and a carton of eggs were sitting next to the gas range. Carl.

He threw away the rotted food and took the liner from the trash can outside. He came back in and pulled the table back to where it was before and set the salt and pepper shakers upright. He looked around for any other signs of Carl that might upset Monica. He grabbed a sponge from the sink, wet it, and wiped grease splatter from around the stove-top burners.

He turned on the hot water, hoping to clean the sponge. He waited a minute and the water turned hot. He was glad she had a gas water heater. A gas water heater? They could shower!

Monica came in to the kitchen and Trey looked at her closely for signs of emotional trauma.

"Are you okay?"

"I'm fine," she said, but didn't quite sound fine. She spoke quietly and pursed her lips, drawing them into her mouth. Just seeing her try to be strong made Trey feel awful inside. He wished for the hundredth time that he could turn back time. "Did you find anything to eat?"

"Not really. I sure wish I had a Sausage McMuffin right about now." He laughed, wondering if or when that would ever be possible again.

"Maybe someday I can make you a veggie sausage muffin." Trey wrinkled his nose at the thought of veggie sausage. "You'd like it. It's really good."

"If you say so," he replied.

"I don't have much food. I decided not to go shopping until after the storm had passed. Everything in the fridge will be ruined by now." She walked over to the cabinet where she kept snack food and pulled out a bag of seaweed puffs.

Trey looked at the bag and said, "I'll just wait till we get to my folk's cabin. I'm not that hungry."

Monica laughed and said, "Try one," lifting a green puff toward his mouth. He reluctantly opened his mouth and let her put it in. He chewed it, looking like she had just fed him a cockroach, then his expression changed.

"This is alright," he said, surprised. She smiled and held the bag out toward him. He took a handful. "I'm eager to get going, but if you don't mind, I'd love to take a quick shower."

"That's a great idea. But you need to be careful. Use my hair cover. It's above the shower head."

After Trey showered, he found that Monica had hung some clothes for him on the doorknob. He got dressed and thought maybe he'd be able to go to the market further down the mountain for a razor and a comb sometime soon. After he came out wearing Thomas's clean clothes, Monica went in and showered.

With both of them looking like clean and well-dressed violent crime victims, they went outside and climbed into the RV and headed south.

***

Tori found the turn-off for the Bunny Lodge and couldn't wait to get there, hoping to find people. When she reached the parking lot, she was excited to see two cars parked there, but then she saw the boarded up windows on the lodge and frowned, not sure what to think.

"Are people here, Mommy?"

"I don't know yet, honey. We'll find out." She went around the car and released Liz from her car seat and lifted her out. "Hold my hand, baby."

Liz took her mother's hand and they walked to the front door. Liz tried to skip but her mother wouldn't match her pace by skipping along with her. Tori thought about how Liz knew nothing of what had happened. She hoped that if they did find people that they wouldn't traumatize her with morbid talk of mass death.

She stopped when she reached the door and just stared at it for a few seconds.

"Come on, Mommy. Why aren't you knocking?"

Tori took a deep breath, let it out and knocked on the door, unconsciously squeezing Liz's hand a little harder.

"Mr. Stepp, I think someone's at your door," Bo called out toward the kitchen where Terry had gone to see what he could come up with for breakfast for five.

Terry came out wearing a cook's apron. "What's that?" he asked.

"Someone at your door."

Bo and Geraldine had slept on the floor close to the fire. They had hoped their clothes would dry as they slept, but they hadn't.

"I'll be right back," Terry said. "Don't open it," he instructed before heading down the hall and knocking on Jim's door. "Jim, we got company."

Jim was half-asleep when Terry knocked. He quickly got up and yawned. He grabbed the .45 from the top of a file cabinet and opened his door. "Company?" he asked.

"Yeah. Bo said someone was knocking on the door."

"Shit," Jim said and rubbed his eyes with his free hand. "Well, let's go."

They walked back to the main room and took up the same positions as the night before when the mother and son had arrived.

"Who's there?" Terry called out.

Tori looked at Liz and they smiled at each other. "My name is Tori, and I have my daughter with me."

Terry looked at Jim and Jim nodded. Terry held his gun behind his back. If it was just a woman and her child, he didn't want to frighten the child. He looked at Jim and gestured for him to do the same. Jim put his gun behind his back and blinked sleep out of his eyes.

"We need a guard shack at the highway turn off," he grumbled as Terry pulled the door open.

"Hello," Terry said when he saw Tori. He quickly glanced to the right and saw that they were alone and that there was a new car in the parking lot. He looked down at Liz, smiling. "What's your name, sweetheart?"

"Wizzabiff," she replied.

Terry laughed and said, "Come inside, Wizzabiff."

Liz glared at him and pouted.

"It's Elizabeth," Tori clarified.

"I'm sorry, Elizabeth. Won't you come in? I was just about to make breakfast. Are you hungry?" Liz nodded.

"Thank you so much, Mister…"

"My name is Terry. Terry Stepp. And this is my friend, Jim." He realized that he didn't know Jim or Angela's last names. "What's your last name, Jim?"

Jim looked at Terry and said, "Ecklund." Both of them tucked their guns into their waistbands and covered them with their shirts as Tori and Liz came inside.

Terry shut the door and bolted it. "You can have a seat at the table. I'll have some food out in just a minute. That's Bo and Geraldine over there." They were sitting up now and working out kinks after sleeping on the wood floor.

Tori said, "Hello" and Liz just glanced at them and stepped closer to her mother.

"Hello, child," Geraldine said and patted her hair with her hands, finding that the cloth napkin she had used as a scarf had fallen back. She untied it, then replaced it on her head and tied it again. "Where is your father?" she asked, raising her eyebrows.

Tori looked at the woman without speaking. She didn't like the look on the woman's face and she didn't think her question was appropriate to be asking a little girl - especially one she didn't know.

"That's really none of your business," Jim said on her behalf. Tori turned to Jim with gratitude in her eyes. She walked over to him with Liz trailing close behind.

"Hi, Jim. My name is Tori. And this is Liz." Jim shook Tori's hand and then reached down to shake Elizabeth's hand, but she wrapped her arms around Tori's leg.

"It's nice to meet you, Tori and Liz. Don't worry about them. They're leaving after breakfast." Jim glanced at Geraldine briefly.

Geraldine and Bo had moved to the hearth where they had sat the night before until Terry had brought them blankets and pillows.

"How long have you worked here, Mr. Ecklund?" Geraldine asked Jim.

"Why do you ask?" he responded, matching her permanent scowl with one of his own.

"How about Mr. Steppe? He said this is his place; I was just wondering if he had any proof of that, like some identification. Because if not, then I don't see why my son and I should have to leave at all."

"I think you should leave right now," Jim said.

"I think we should have a talk with Mr. Stepp," Geraldine replied.

Jim and Geraldine glared at each other. Bo looked back and forth from his mother to Jim. Angela came walking into the room and didn't like the look on Jim's face. She could tell that Jim was glaring at Geraldine and wondered what had happened now. Then she saw Tori and Liz and she stopped.

"New people," she said. Liz smiled at Angela.

"Hi there, cutie. What's your name?" Angela walked to within a few feet of Liz and dropped to her knees.

"Wizzabiff."

"Well hello, Elizabeth. I'm so happy to meet you. When did you get here?"

Liz shrugged and looked up at her mother.

"Hi. I'm Tori - Liz's mother. It's nice to meet you. But it looks like we came at a bad time." She shifted her eyes toward the hearth without moving her head. Angela nodded lightly.

"Why don't you guys have a seat and I'll find us something to eat." She looked at Liz. "Are you hungry, sweetheart?"

Liz nodded solemnly.

"Terry's getting something," Jim said.

Angela walked over to Jim and embraced him, whispering, "What's going on?"

Jim whispered back, "They need to leave before I lose it. I can't take another minute of that hag."

"Let's see if Terry needs some help bringing stuff out," Angela said, pulling Jim with her to the kitchen. "We'll be right back," she said, smiling at Tori and Liz.

Tori pulled two chairs out from the table. She picked Liz up and deposited her in one of the chairs and scooted it close to the table, then sat next to her. Their backs were to the hearth and Tori felt like she was being rude, but she also felt that the woman had started it.

Jim and Angela entered the kitchen where Terry was trying to fit two boxes of cereal, six bowls stacked three high, and a gallon of milk on one serving tray.

"I totally forgot we had milk!" Angela said.

"It was frozen, but it thawed out while it rained. You guys left all of the new people out there alone?"

"I woke up from Jim raising his voice to Geraldine, so I brought him back here to calm him down."

"Don't worry. I'm eating in the kitchen. Terry, will you please take them away after they eat?" Jim glared at the kitchen door as if he could see through it to where Geraldine was sitting. "She wants proof that you own the resort. She thinks she's staying. Said we don't have the right to make her leave."

"Well, we don't, technically speaking, other than squatter's rights. We were here first. Let me get this out there and we'll figure out how to get them to leave gracefully. Angela, could you bring the milk?" He picked up the tray and headed toward the door. Angela followed him out.

"They took my bowl," Jim said to himself. He waited and when the door to the kitchen opened, Angela came through carrying two bowls and two spoons. He smiled at her and went to the pantry to get another box of cereal. They sat down at a small table against a wall where Terry's radio played static noise at a low volume.

Jim ate silently, still brooding over Geraldine and the nerve of the woman. Why would she even want to stay in a place where she wasn't welcome, he wondered.

"I don't suppose there's any chance of you and Geraldine working things out and starting over?"

Jim looked up at her with his head over his bowl, spooning cereal into his mouth.

"I didn't think so. We never really considered this possibility; letting people in and then deciding they don't fit in with us very well." Jim looked at her again. "Or not at all," she finished.

"That woman is a glaring example of the worst that Christianity has to offer," Jim finally said. "She's got her head buried as far as it can go into the bible, but she makes sure not to let it get anywhere near her heart."

Eleven

It was the mattress in the window that drew Carl's attention. He knew he was close, but none of the cabins looked familiar. He and Trey had only been here once, and Trey found that his key no longer worked. His father changed the locks as he had threatened to do to keep Trey out.

When Carl saw the mattress in the broken window, he slowed down and thought he recognized the place. He pulled into the driveway, checked the blood on the diaper and was pleased to see that the bleeding was still minor. He got out and walked up to the door. This was definitely the place. He remembered the stupid little plaque attached to the wall above the mailbox that said, "Thank you, Mr. Postman."

He tried the door and found it locked. He stepped over to the window and pushed the mattress. The top half folded inward, but the bottom resisted and stayed in place. He put the bottom of his boot low on the mattress and pushed forward. Now it moved. He kept pushing at it until he created a gap big enough to fit through.

He climbed in the window and sidestepped to the left until he was past the mattress and saw that a couch was holding the mattress in place. Someone must've broken in and gotten creative to keep the cold air out. The inside of the cabin was warm and there was a fire burning.

He was suddenly alert realizing that Trey could be here even though there wasn't a car in the driveway. He pulled the .22 from his waistband and looked around, listening for any signs of occupancy. He could see the dining room to his left, so he stepped carefully forward toward a doorway that would be the likely place for Trey to be sleeping.

He crept up on the room and looked inside. It was empty. This was where the mattress had come from. There was another door adjacent to the front door. He walked slowly and quietly over to that door and carefully turned the knob without making a sound. He raised his gun, ready to fire and pushed the door open quickly.

Another empty room. He thought this one was probably a garage that got converted. It looked like a taxidermy studio with stuffed animals scattered around the room and a workbench with a bunch of tools and supplies neatly lined up on it. Carl went to the kitchen and confirmed that it was empty too.

A grocery sack on the table looked out of place and got his attention. He walked over and saw something written on it. He moved the sugar bowl and read the writing.

Mom, Dad or Trey,

Liz and I were here. Sorry about the window. We're going to check out the Bunny Lodge for people and/or supplies. Running out of food here.

We hope you're all okay and we'll see you soon!

Tori

Carl smiled an evil grin. He hadn't found Trey yet, but now he knew where to find his sister. That was even better. Revenge was definitely going to be sweet now. He'd never spoken to her, but he'd seen her once as Trey argued with her outside of her work. As he recalled, she was a hot little number, and he thought she might be a nurse too. Carl started laughing, imagining how things could turn out. He'd get Tori to take care of him, and then he'd take care of her.

"Oh boy. You never should've fucked with me, Trey. Your sister is gonna pay for your sins, you backstabbing bastard." Carl laughed again, loving the way life surprised him sometimes. He dropped the bag and went to the front door; unlocking it and leaving it open as he walked out.

Damn. It was snowing again. Well, at least he had a car with a roof now. And windshield wipers. He got in the car being careful with his shoulder and headed down the road back to the highway.

Just when Carl started to doubt if he actually knew where the Bunny Lodge was, he saw the sign for the resort with an arrow pointing to the right. He took the turn a little too fast and the car slid. He told himself to slow down. He was nearly there. He didn't need to go crashing the damn car now when he was so close to getting some payback.

The road was on an incline and he lost traction occasionally but he regained it by letting up on the gas. Fucking snow. This resort would be a good place to wait out the winter. Much better than the abandoned resort he usually crashed in when he was on the mountain and had nowhere to go. Maybe he'd let Tori stay alive until spring. She'd make a good bed warmer. Carl was smiling as he crested the hill and made the turn into the parking lot. His smile disappeared when he saw two cars and a truck already there.

He hadn't thought about the possibility of other people being at the lodge. That fucked things up, at least for the time being. He'd have to find out what the situation was before he could plan his revenge and his fun. Maybe he'd be real lucky and the place would be filled with women. He could have a harem for the winter.

He parked next to a faggot yuppie car which made his station wagon look like the piece of shit that it was. He told himself that it was possible that a rich bitch was driving the BMW. But if it belonged to a man, it probably wasn't one he needed to be too worried about. He thought for a minute, preparing himself mentally for how he would approach Tori and whoever was inside with her.

He tried to imagine himself feeling sad and needing help; just a harmless guy who was wounded and scared and didn't have anywhere to turn; glad to have found people after what he'd been through. Carl ran the scenario and the character through his mind for a moment longer, then got out of the car and put the .22 in his right front pants pocket.

He walked slowly to the door, trying to look wounded and weak in case anyone was watching him. He held his left arm with his right hand and grimaced as if he was in pain. He actually was in pain, but he focused on it and imagined that it was much worse than it was. He knocked on the door without using much force.

"Is anybody there? I need help!" he cried out in a voice higher pitched than his normal tone.

Terry scooted his chair back and rushed to the kitchen.

"We've got more company. Come on," Terry said poking his head into the kitchen, then he let go of the kitchen door and went back into the main room. Jim got up and went through the door after him.

"What do you mean? More?"

"Someone's at the door."

"Jesus Christ!"

Geraldine hissed as he walked past her. "How dare you take His name in--?"

"Shut the fuck up," Jim growled.

Terry and Jim got into what had become their standard positions at the door. They pulled their guns out and Jim nodded at Terry, signaling that he was ready.

***

Trey slowed to a crawl as he carefully turned the big RV into the driveway at his parent's cabin. It was much too long and it stuck out into the street, but he figured there wouldn't be any traffic anyway, so he didn't worry about it. Besides, the fact that the driveway was empty almost guaranteed that Tori wasn't here, so they wouldn't be staying long anyway.

Everything here looked wrong to him. The front door was standing open and he could see snow covering the first few feet of the floor inside the doorway. Plus someone had broken the big front window. What was a mattress doing there? Trey didn't like this. It was bad enough that someone had broken in, but what had they done while they were in there? He and Monica picked up their handguns from the center console and opened their doors. Trey waited for Monica to come around to his side.

"I don't like this. Stay behind me, just in case."

She raised her gun. "I'm armed too. Don't worry about me."

Trey approached the doorway cautiously. He leaned into the doorway and looked around. Straight across from him he could see the foot of the king size bed's box spring. He went forward to look in that room first. No one was in there. The blankets had been removed along with the mattress.

He checked his dad's work room. It was empty and looked undisturbed. Who'd want to steal taxidermy stuff anyway, he thought. There were embers burning in the fireplace. If someone was here, they weren't doing a good job of keeping the fire going.

He went forward, turned right and saw couch cushions on the floor along with the blankets from the bedroom. There was also an empty grocery sack on the floor. He went in a little further and saw that the kitchen was empty.

"No one's here. And I know my parents didn't do this. Someone broke in and stayed here for a while, but they're gone now."

Monica looked in the kitchen and saw a big metal pot on the floor half filled with water.

"Do you mind if we take that pot? We can use it to melt snow in."

"Go ahead. My folks ain't gonna miss it."

Monica picked up the pot and drained the water in the sink as Trey went back into the living room to puzzle over the broken window, the couch and the mattress. As Monica left the kitchen she stopped to pick up the paper sack and opened it to put the pot inside. She noticed the writing on it.

"Trey, come here. Your sister left a note!"

"What?" Trey rushed over and read his sister's writing on the sack. "She was here!" A smile lit up his face. "She's alive! Oh my God. She and Liz are okay. And they're not far from here. We gotta go find them."

When they reached the turn for the Bunny Lodge, Trey slowed the RV to a stop and looked deep in thought.

"What is it, Trey?"

"All the way from the cabin, we've been following a single set of tracks, and they turn here, going to the lodge, just like we are."

"Well, yeah. They're probably your sister's tracks."

"My sister wasn't the one who broke into the cabin. She'd have the new key."

"So what are you saying?"

"Someone could've come here specifically looking for her. What if it was Carl who broke into the cabin, looking for us?"

Monica's mouth dropped open. "He could have your sister!"

"That's what I was thinking."

Twelve

Terry opened the door a little and peeked out through a one inch gap. He saw a man standing there with a badly bruised face, looking like he was in great pain. He pulled the door open wider.

"Thank you, sir. I need help. I've been shot," Carl said, turning to his right to show the bullet wound on the left side of his back.

Terry looked back at Jim for his consent to let the stranger in. Jim took a breath, puffed out his cheeks as he exhaled, nodding and looking weary.

"Come inside," Terry said, stepping back to make room for the man to enter. "What happened to you?"

"I was mugged," Carl said. He came in, dragging his feet as though he barely had the strength to walk. As he entered the lodge, he rapidly glanced around the room, taking in the occupants, their genders, and the fact that the guy who opened the door and another, younger guy were armed. Everyone but the two guys was sitting at a long dining table, mostly near the center. He spotted Tori sitting next to a little kid. "Does anyone here have any medical experience?"

Geraldine and Tori both got up and came over to Carl who collapsed to his knees and reached out for the table to keep from falling any further. Jim had seen Carl's eyes darting around the room and felt suspicious about him.

He may be wounded, but his mind is alert and he knows exactly what he's doing, Jim thought.

"My mother served in the WACS in the Philippines. She taught me a lot of emergency first aid when she came back," Geraldine said.

Elizabeth tried to imagine an old woman's mother in wax. She couldn't do it.

"I'm a CNA and studying to be a nurse," Tori said.

"Bring us whatever first aid supplies you have, and since I'm sure no one has forceps, maybe you can find a pair of needle-nose pliers. Alcohol too, if you have any," Geraldine said.

Jim asked Terry, "Do you have the keys to the lounge?"

"No. They're in the manager's office, hanging up."

Jim left to get the keys and some alcohol.

"Terry, can you boil a pot of water as fast as you can?" Tori asked.

"Sure." Terry trotted to the kitchen.

As Jim came walking back through the main room with the keys to the lounge, Geraldine asked if there was a table or something elevated where they could lay Carl.

Jim said there was a large desk in the manager's office. "Just clear off the stuff and put him there. Angela can show you where it is." A crisis seems to bring out the best in her, Jim thought.

"Follow me. I'll clear off the desk," Angela said, heading down the hall, passing the offices that Terry and Jim used for bedrooms and turning into a room on the right that had a gold-tinted plaque on the door that said MANAGER. She removed a desk blotter, pen holder, stapler and phone, putting them all on the office chair and rolling it back out of the way.

Carl walked in, supported on either side by Geraldine and Tori. They walked him to the desk and Tori asked him to lie face down. He did, feeling the discomfort of the gun in his pocket, but there was nothing he could do about it yet.

"We'll need to take off your shirt," Geraldine said. "You need to keep your left arm still. Angela, look in the desk for some scissors."

Angela pulled open the large center drawer and found scissors in a plastic tray along with an Exacto knife, a staple remover, staples and paperclips. She handed the scissors to Geraldine who carefully cut away Carl's shirt.

Jim came in and put a bottle of Seagram's Seven and a bottle of Bacardi 151 on a filing cabinet. He couldn't believe that Geraldine frowned in disapproval at the bottles of alcohol, even though she was the one who asked for them. *Crazy*, he thought.

Jim went back to the main room and saw Terry come out of the kitchen walking slowly and carefully as he carried a pot of water with steam rising from it. Elizabeth was standing by the table pouting. She had been left alone in the main room with Bo, who she was afraid of because he was so big and he never talked.

Terry spoke as he passed by Jim. "There's a guy talking on the short-wave! He said only Denver and Colorado Springs were hit with nukes and the feds have a terrorist cell member in custody who says this is only the beginning."

"Holy shit!"

"I'll be right back after I get this water to the women."

Jim went over to Liz and said, "While your mommy is busy being a hero, would you like to listen to the radio with me?"

Liz looked around and considered that the only alternative was to sit with the big silent man, so she slid out of her chair and walked toward Jim who she thought was much nicer.

Jim took her by the hand and led her to the kitchen. Terry came in a moment later and dragged a metal stool over to the table and sat down.

Two men on the radio were talking to each other via shortwave. The one currently speaking sounded like a young Asian-American.

"Normally, they don't say anything but 'Death to America' when they get caught. The fact that this guy is talking makes me think he may be telling the truth."

"Homeland Security said his threats are baseless. He's just blowin' smoke," said another guy with a New England accent.

"Of course they would say that! They don't want people to panic."

"I can accept a couple jihadis nuking Colorado, but do you seriously think North Korea and Iran could follow up with additional strikes? And even if they could, why haven't they?"

"Don't forget, he also said Russia and China were uncommitted. So they might decide to join the alliance against us."

"There is no alliance against us. This was nothing more than a couple of goat-fuckers who got lucky. And all they managed to do was kill a bunch of people in Colorado. They didn't take our defense systems down like they intended, so even if there is a bigger alliance against us, things didn't go as planned."

"Only because we have Cheyenne Mountain on stand-by, otherwise we wouldn't... Shit, shit, shit! Harold, is your TV on?"

"Ayuh. I'm watchin' the game. Why? Oh my God! Emergency Alert System just came on and knocked the game off the air!"

In the lodge kitchen, they could faintly hear the discordant two-tone signal in the background of one of the men's houses.

The Asian-American screamed into his mic, "Holy fuck! Did you hear that? They said, 'Don't be alarmed,' but get to a bomb shelter! Right! I'm fucking alarmed, dude!"

The kitchen door swung open. Bo ducked down and poked his head in.

"There's someone here. I figured ya'll would wanna take up your positions by the door like you been doin'."

Jim asked Liz to wait right there until he came back and to listen to the "show" on the radio. He and Terry headed to the main door and ran into Angela entering the room from the hall.

"I think I heard a truck, or something big pull up," she said.

"Yeah. We know. This place is Grand Fucking Central today," Jim said as he went past her heading toward the door. "How's that guy doing?"

"Tori actually managed to get the bullet out and Geraldine is stitching him up. I couldn't watch. I don't know how anyone can do that, but I'm glad that some people can."

"A guy on the radio said that nukes only hit Denver and Colorado Springs; most likely they wanted the Peterson base, but –" Jim started to say.

"So we can go home?" Angela asked, very excited.

"But there may be more on the way. We don't know yet. And Liz is in the kitchen by herself."

"Oh... I'll go sit with her." Angela's excitement was short-lived. She turned left toward the kitchen thinking of how wonderful it would be to go home and to have electricity, and her cell phone, and the internet. Relief washed over her as she realized that her family and friends were all alive.

Bo walked over to the fireplace to get out of a possible line of fire. Terry and Jim waited for a knock.

Thirteen

"That's Tori's car," Trey said. "I wonder what Carl's driving since he left his bike at your house."

"What do you think we should do?" Monica asked.

"I think the only thing we *can* do is go in with guns in the open and tell him we're taking Tori and Liz and he ain't stopping us."

"What if he has a gun?"

"He probably does, knowing him. But I don't think he wants to get shot. There's two of us and one of him."

"And whoever else is in there with him," Monica said, looking at the other cars in the parking lot.

"I don't think his gang is here. Not with a BMW, a pickup truck with no bike in the back, and a station wagon. I'm going in. You can stay here and wait if you want. In fact, I think it would be better if you did."

"Are you kidding me? If Carl's in there, I want to see him. It's not over between me and him." She pulled the slide back on her gun, loading a round into the chamber.

"Okay." Trey put his Glock in his waistband and picked up the shotgun. He racked it and a shell flew toward the dining area. "Damn. This thing was all set to go." He fetched the shell and loaded it back into the shotgun. "I'm ready when you are."

"Trey, if anything happens, I just want to thank you again for helping me."

"Nothing's gonna happen to us."

They got out of the RV and started walking to the lodge. Trey walked a little faster, trying to stay in front of Monica.

Terry heard the RV doors shut and said, "I guess they finally decided to come and visit. I should cut some peep holes in this wood so we can see outside."

"Yeah. Blinding us to potential threats probably wasn't one of your better ideas," Jim replied.

The knock they'd been waiting for finally came.

"Who's there?" Terry called out.

"I'm lookin' for my sister, Tori. She told me I'd find her here."

Terry turned and nodded at Jim. He had no problem with letting the guy in. Jim nodded back. Terry opened the door and quickly raised his pistol and yelled, "Gun!" as he backed away from the door and aimed at Trey's head.

"Hey, hey! It's okay," Trey said, raising his shotgun above his head horizontally. "I'm just carrying this for self-defense. I don't mean you no harm. We've been through some hell lately."

Terry could see that both of them looked like they'd been beaten pretty badly and the guy looked and sounded sincere. He lowered his weapon. "Come in, but put that on the mantel. There's a child in here."

"Is it my niece, Lizzie?" Trey asked as he walked over to the fireplace and laid the shotgun down on the mantel. Monica put her gun behind her back while Trey was assuring Terry that he wasn't a threat. She didn't intend to put it down or give it up.

Angela and Liz came through the kitchen door. When Liz saw Trey, she ran toward him with a big smile. "Uncle Trey! Uncle Trey!" She was glad to see someone she knew after being cooped up in her grandparent's cabin for a week.

Angela came over and introduced herself to Trey and Monica. Everyone in the room except for Bo gave their names and shook hands.

"Angie, any news on the radio?'

"Jim, there's been nothing on the radio but static."

"Mommy!" Liz ran toward the long hall. Tori and Geraldine were coming down the hall. Tori stopped and scooped Liz into her arms.

"We're all done, baby. I hope you've been good." Tori froze. A woman she'd never seen before was pointing a gun at her. She slowly put Liz down and said, "Go to one of the rooms behind me. Any one of them. Now!"

"Step aside!" Monica yelled. Tori looked behind her and saw Carl reach down and pick Liz up with his right hand. He shifted her over to support her weight on his left hip and wrapped his left arm around her. He pulled his gun out of his pocket with his right hand and pointed it at Liz's head."

Jim and Terry drew their guns. Trey ran to the fireplace and got his shotgun and ran back to Monica's side.

"Let her go, Carl!" Trey yelled.

"I don't know what the hell's going on here, but everyone needs to put down their weapons and just calm the fuck down. And you, put that shotgun down," Jim said.

Trey remembered he also had a pistol, so he placed the shotgun on the dining table behind Monica. He pulled out his pistol and aimed it at Carl.

"Tori and the kid are comin' with me," Carl said to the group of people pointing firearms at him. "Let us out of here and no one gets hurt."

"That ain't gonna happen, Carl. Your reign of terror ends here. You put my niece down, now. If anything happens to her, so help me God…I'll make sure you die slowly."

Tori had her back against the wall. Her heart was thundering in her chest as she stood only a few feet from her daughter. "I just worked to save your life," she said to Carl.

"Ain't nothin' personal, Tori. Your brother done brought this on."

"How about leaving my little girl out of it?" Tori said, breaking into tears. "Please! Let her go."

"Everyone just back away and make a path to the door!" Carl yelled.

No one moved, then suddenly Geraldine stepped forward out of the group in the main room and started toward the hall.

"In the name of the Lord, I compel you to release that child! In Jesus' name, I command you, devil!"

Carl fired his .22 and Geraldine stopped and stood still. Blood oozed out of a small hole between her eyebrows. Her knees stopped working and she collapsed. Angela ran to the kitchen for safety and to get away from the dead body bleeding from the head.

"Momma!" Bo yelled, bolting from the hearth and coming to her side. He kneeled down and saw the dead stare in her eyes. He got up slowly and turned toward Carl. Liz was screaming and struggling to get free.

Tori held her arms stretched out toward her daughter, crying, "Please, let her go. Please, Carl."

There was ten feet of hallway between Bo and Carl. Bo suddenly got up and flew down the hall with his arms out in front of him, reaching for Carl's throat.

Carl fired once as the big man flew toward him with impossible speed. Bo closed the distance between them in two seconds and knocked him backwards as he closed his hands around Carl's neck. Carl fired as he fell, his shots going wild. He let go of Liz to break his fall with his left hand. Tori went to grab Liz and was hit by one of Carl's stray shots. She picked up her daughter and ran with her to the manager's office.

Carl was making a choking sound, trying to pull Bo's hands off his throat with his left hand and turning the gun in his right hand to point it at Bo. He fired repeatedly, finally hitting Bo with his last two bullets. When Carl heard his pistol dry-fire, he started hitting Bo's left arm with the gun.

Terry and Jim grabbed Bo's arms and pulled him backwards off of Carl. "That's enough, Bo," Terry yelled. "Let him go." Bo reluctantly released his grip on Carl's throat and started to cry. They released him and he crawled back to his mother's body, leaving a trail of blood from his bullet wounds. He collapsed next to her and wrapped a bleeding arm around her.

Carl quickly picked up the gun and tried to stand up, coughing and choking. His face was red and he had thumb imprints on his throat. He couldn't talk yet. He just waved his gun side to side at Jim and Terry, gesturing for them to get out of his way.

"His gun's empty," Trey said.

Jim and Terry stepped out of Carl's way while keeping their guns trained on him. They looked at Trey and Monica who stood side by side also aiming their guns at Carl.

"Your gun's empty, Carl. It's over. You've done all the harm you're gonna do in this life."

Carl dropped the empty pistol. "Are you gonna shoot an unarmed man, Trey?"

"God knows you deserve it, but I ain't like you, Carl. I don't know what we're gonna do with you, but I ain't gonna shoot you in cold blood."

"I am."

A shot rang out and Carl jerked back a step and grabbed his stomach. Blood seeped out between his fingers. Everyone turned to look at Monica and saw smoke drifting off the barrel of her gun.

"Go ahead, bitch. Finish me off!" Carl yelled.

"No. I like Trey's idea of you dying slowly," she said.

Jim looked at Terry, not sure what to do next. "What the hell?"

"I don't know what's going on here" Terry said. "But I know one thing; Tori probably isn't going to help you again after you held a gun to her little girl's head. And you killed the only other person who might've been able to save your life."

"Why did you shoot him?" Jim asked Monica.

"He beat me and raped me," she answered so quietly they could barely hear her voice.

Jim put his gun in his back pocket and then grabbed Carl and forced him toward the door.

"Where are you taking me?"

"Outside," Jim replied.

"What the hell for?"

"So you can die cold and alone like you deserve. Plus you're getting blood all over my nice clean floor."

Terry ran to the door and opened it. Jim shoved Carl through the doorway, slammed the door and locked it.

Carl fell to the ground and stayed there for a minute, unable to move due to the pain in his stomach. They all thought he was going to die, but they were wrong. He'd survive this and he'd come back and kill every one of them. He was tougher than they thought.

He summoned his strength and stood up. It hurt less when he was standing, so he decided he'd be better off just walking away instead of driving. He walked across the lot and turned onto the road.

He didn't know where he was going or what he was going to do next. He held his right hand on his stomach and focused on taking one step after another. The more he walked, the less he felt the pain. He looked down and was pleasantly surprised to see that the bleeding from his stomach had slowed.

He began to laugh, thinking he was actually going to be okay. He reached the highway and had to make a decision about which way to go. As he tried to recall which way would get him to shelter the quickest, he heard the sound of an engine coming around a bend in the road.

The timing was perfect. He could catch a ride. The Lord truly did provide. He saw a white Ford F350 come into view. He pulled his right hand away from his gunshot wound and put his left hand in its place. He waved his right arm at the truck and smiled when he saw it slow down and veer gradually to the side, pulling over for him.

The bearded driver got out first and walked quickly toward Carl. Then the other doors opened and four more men got out. One of them shouted, "Hold up, Noah! There's a proper ritual for blood atonement. You can't just go up and slit his throat on the side of the road."

"Watch me," Noah replied.

###

Epilogue

Jim, Angela, Terry, Trey, Monica, Tori and Elizabeth lived together in the lodge without further incident (aside from some minor jealousy on Angela's part when she felt her budding relationship with Jim was threatened by Tori's presence.)

The four graves they left behind were unmarked and the burials were unceremonious. Tori's gunshot was only a flesh wound and she recovered quickly. Liz had a bump on her head and a sprained arm but was otherwise unharmed. Tori was unable to remove the bullets from Bo's lung and he died the following day.

The Emergency Alert System heard over the shortwave radio was activated due to incoming missiles detected by the Alternate Command Center on stand-by in Cheyenne Mountain and the Alaskan Norad Region. Recent budget cuts in defense spending rendered the U.S. incapable of a defensive response. The president declined to counter-attack despite being urged to do so by military commanders who ultimately decided they had nothing at all to lose by defying their commander in chief and his orders to stand-down.

Despite additional pre-programmed missiles which struck the already devastated cities of Denver and Colorado Springs, as well as every major city in America, the occupants of the Bunny Lodge were physically unaffected as they avoided fallout by staying inside, not even venturing out for food from their cold storage.

No additional visitors arrived at the lodge, and after the end of winter, the group headed south in a small convoy to find a suitable place to grow food and to start a new life in what was left of America.

About the author

Edward M. Wolfe is an author and a musician. His short story, "When Everything Changed," appears in the 2014 Word Branch Science Fiction Anthology "Nascence" He is also a songwriter and plays guitar.

The author enjoys hearing from readers and can be reached at ewolfe@outlook.com. He appreciates reader reviews and invites you to visit http://EdwardMWolfe.com where you can enjoy free micro-short stories and non-fiction essays and sign up to be informed of new releases. His books can be viewed at http://amazon.com/author/edwolfe

Made in the USA
Charleston, SC
09 January 2014